THE DRAGON'S CHOICE

Tahoe Dragon Mates #1

JESSIE DONOVAN

Mythical Lake Press, LLC

This book is a work of fiction. Names, characters, places, and incidents are either the product of the writer's imagination or are used fictitiously, and any resemblance to actual persons, living or dead, business establishments, events, or locales is entirely coincidental.

The Dragon's Choice

Books in this series:

·~

The Dragon's Choice Synopsis

After Jose Santos's younger sister secretly enters them both into the yearly dragon lottery and they get selected, he begrudgingly agrees to participate. It means picking a human female from a giant room full of them and staying around just long enough to get her pregnant. However, when his dragon notices one female who keeps hiding behind a book, Jose has a new plan—win his fated mate, no matter what it takes.

Victoria Lewis prefers being home with a book and away from large crowds. But she desperately wants to study dragon-shifters at close range, so she musters up her courage to enter the dragon lottery. When she's selected as one of the potential candidates, she decides to accept her spot. After all, it's not as if the dragon-shifter will pick her—an introverted bookworm who prefers jeans and sweats to skirts or fancy clothes. Well, until he's standing right in front of her with flashing eyes and says he wants her.

As Jose tries to win his fated female, trouble stirs inside his clan. Will he be able to keep his mate with him forever? Or will the American Department of Dragon Affairs whisk her away to some other clan to protect her?

NOTE: This is a quick, steamy standalone story about fated mates and sexy dragon-shifters near Lake Tahoe in the USA. You don't have to read all my other dragon books to enjoy this one!

Chapter One

Jose Santos waited inside a small room, one adjacent to the ballroom of the human hotel, and resisted the urge to run.

He'd never understood why people wanted to live cheek and jowl among thousands, with concrete and pavement covering the ground and banishing most of nature. Despite having worked with the humans in the US Forest Service for over a decade, he still barely understood them.

And yet here he was, inside a hotel in South Lake Tahoe, about ready to pick a human female at random to hopefully impregnate and increase his kind.

His inner dragon—the second personality inside his head—spoke up. *Remember, you can't fuck this up today or you'll dash Gaby's dreams.*

Ah, yes. Gabriela, the little sister who had entered them both into the yearly lottery, one she couldn't enter herself since it had to be all the unmated siblings in a family or nothing. *Considering she didn't ask my permission, I'm being pretty fucking generous just being here.*

You had the chance to back out last month, but you didn't. And we both know why.

Damn dragon, knowing too much.

Every dragon-shifter lived to find their true mate, the one that stirred their inner beast and kicked off a mate-claim frenzy when kissed.

However, despite the millions of visitors that came to the greater Lake Tahoe area every year, Jose had never so much as glimpsed at a female who urged him to do more than growl and tell them to leave him the hell alone.

He had no tolerance for the dragon groupies that came to the lake to try to find a dragon-shifter to kiss or fuck. Entire tourist companies had grown around such a goal. He was surprised the human government hadn't stepped in to intervene, especially since, in recent years, it'd forced most of the dragon clans in the area to keep more and more to themselves to avoid the hassle.

Not that dealing with the groupies was his problem to solve. Jose only wanted the chance to spot his true mate, and this lottery gave him a chance to really look at a group of humans without having to run and avoid females throwing themselves at him.

His inner dragon snorted. *That one who jumped off a boat, to try and land on us as we floated in the lake, deserved some points for originality.*

No, it was pure stupidity. She couldn't swim, and we had to save her. And we're not the only ones who've had to dodge them like bullets.

His beast huffed. *Well, you can't complain too much about today, then. The rules won't allow the females to run or jump on us.*

Which is the only reason I'm here.

True, while the chances of her being inside the next room were slim to say the least, it was worth the time to look, even if his true mate ended up being human, which wasn't his first choice.

And even if she wasn't here, then he should at least get a few fun fucks out of it—ones where he controlled the situation—so it wasn't a complete loss.

An employee from the American Department of Dragon Affairs—or ADDA—barged into the room. Even though the female was short and would probably blow over if Jose breathed too hard, she stood tall and didn't wither at his hard expression. Good thing, too, as these lotteries tended to work better when the humans in charge weren't afraid.

He'd met her once before and knew her name was Ashley Swift. The human motioned with her hand. "Come on. It's time to get this thing started."

Not moving, Jose asked, "How many are there?"

"About two hundred or so candidates passed the interviews and tests this time."

Two hundred lucky ones, at least according to the humans. Every few years, they held these lotteries in South Lake Tahoe for the surrounding dragon clans, and every time thousands entered. Not all dragon clans in the US were as open to mating or reproducing with humans, but the four Tahoe area clans preferred survival over purity.

Jose rolled his shoulders. "All right, let's do this."

Ashley raised her brows. "You remember the rules, right?"

He sighed. "Of course I do. She has to come willingly, and no kissing until she signs the paperwork. All pretty fucking romantic, isn't it?"

Ashley didn't blink an eye. "Getting her to be willing may be hard for you, Mr. Santos, if you don't at least try to be less intimidating."

He eyed the slip of a woman and leaned close. "Are you sure you don't want to enter?"

She rolled her eyes. "My fiancé would definitely have a word or two to say about that suggestion."

Damn, of course the one human female who didn't treat him like some god would already belong to another. Now if he could just find one like her but unattached, he might actually not dread this.

His dragon murmured, *Plenty exist. Our cousin's friend mated one.*

Yes, but that was in Canada where dragons and humans have much longer histories of understanding and cooperation than in the US.

Ashley turned toward the door. "It's now or never, Mr. Santos. This is the last chance to back out, but it will pull your sister out, too, and disqualify your clan from entering for five years."

Which would mean Gaby wouldn't have her stupid fantasy come true next month.

Jose may be cynical, but he loved his younger sister. So he took a step toward the door, kicking the ADDA employee into motion, and they both entered the ballroom.

The human females were seated in rows, with barely enough space for him to walk down each one without kicking either a chair or someone's legs. Two hundred didn't sound like a lot given more than that stayed in just this one hotel. But with them all lined up, it was an endless sea of faces.

How the hell was he supposed to pick one of them?

His dragon growled. *Stop coming up with excuses. I'm sure one of them will stand out from the rest.*

The ADDA employee stood behind the podium with a microphone and spoke up. "Hello, and welcome to the Lake Tahoe dragon lottery. This year's dragonman is Jose Santos of Clan PineRock. He'll soon roam the room and pick one lucky woman to whisk away to a private cabin and, well, get to business. If for any reason, you wish to drop out, this is your last opportunity to do so. If you back out after you've been chosen, then you'll be banned from entering any other lotteries. And not just in Tahoe, but in the entire country. I'll pause here for those who wish to leave."

Ashley waited for about thirty seconds, but none of the females rose and walked out.

Well, at least they were committed, he had to give them that.

Of course, as many of them eyed him like a piece of candy, ready to be licked, it could just be that they found him sexy, like a walking fantasy.

His dragon snorted. *Was there any doubt about that?*

And people thought Jose's human half was the arrogant one.

Ashely continued once more, preventing Jose from replying to his dragon. "Good, then it seems we have the right bunch for this year. To help things run smoothly, please remain seated where you are and remain silent unless you're asked a question. You can raise your hand to have an ADDA employee come to you, in case of an emergency." She swept a gaze across the room that made even Jose's dragon take notice. "If someone breaks the rules, they'll be disqualified. No exceptions." She gestured toward Jose. "You may begin."

It was on the tip of his tongue to make a sarcastic quip, but he resisted. Ashley was just doing her job, and he *was* here voluntarily. Just because most humans annoyed him didn't mean he had to make a decent one's life difficult.

As Jose walked down one row and then the others, he noted females of all shapes, sizes, and ethnicities, all pretty in their own way. But it soon became a blur of faces. None of them stood out above the rest, screaming for him to talk with them.

He said to his inner beast, *How the hell do I pick one?*

Even if you're only half-heartedly looking, I'm being more thorough. If our true mate is here, I'll find her.

Before he could reply, he noticed a dark-haired female at the very back, a book in front of her face, hiding everything but the crown of her head from view. He stared a second, she peeked over the top to study him, revealing dark eyes before ducking back behind the book.

Her strange behavior made him pause a second and study her more.

Even from thirty feet away he could read the title of the book in front of her face: *Revealing the Dragons: The Day-to-Day Lives of a British Dragon-Shifter Clan.*

It was the famous book about dragon-shifters, the one written a couple years ago by a human female in the UK mated to a dragonman.

Jose had to admit he didn't think anyone would've bothered to study his kind before the lottery since they didn't need to try to win him to get into his pants.

He watched as the female stole a glimpse of him again, her dark brows coming together as if trying to assess something, and then returned her eyes to the book.

Okay, his curiosity was piqued.

While he was supposed to go down the rows in order, he ignored the suggested route and made his way toward the female with the book.

Only when he was right in front of her did she finally gasp and lower the book, revealing her beautiful face. The O shape of her mouth made one side of his own tick up.

Before he could notice more than her dark hair and brown eyes, let alone say anything, his dragon roared. *That's her.*

VICTORIA LEWIS KNEW she should keep her beloved book in the backpack under her chair and try to look sexy to attract the dragonman's notice.

Hell, every woman around her was doing that, some even wearing tops that were little more than bras and skirts that would no doubt show the edges of their asses if they bent over a little.

She resisted looking down at her own outfit. Victoria had worn a simple stretchy bright green V-neck shirt, a color everyone said looked good on her, and jeans. No makeup, no flashy earrings, nothing. She was just herself. Well, mostly. She preferred sweats to jeans, but being close to a dragon-shifter for the first time required a teensy bit of effort.

Not that she expected to be chosen. Victoria was here to sate her curiosity, end of story. The dragonman toward the front of the room was the closest she'd ever gotten to one. Sure, she could've tried joining one of those tours or finding one of the rumored bars where dragon-shifters sometimes hung out.

However, the thought of going into a bar and trying to talk with strangers made her want to run in the opposite direction.

No, the only way for an introvert like her to ever see a dragon-shifter up close like this was at one of these lotteries.

Entering alone had taken her several hours of mustering courage before she could hit Send. And even being accepted had almost made her decline and forget about it.

But then she remembered that if two hundred women gathered into a room, all vying to be the one to win sex with a dragon-shifter, it was highly unlikely the dragon-shifter would pick her.

Oh, Victoria liked herself and didn't really care about how she preferred books to people most of the time, or that her job entailed her working from home on her computer and she could lounge in yoga pants all day.

But dragon-shifters at these lotteries tended to want outgoing women who radiated experience.

Virgin she may not be, but she could count the number of guys on her hand and still not use all the fingers.

So out the book had come, and she'd been checking it against what she saw in person, not wanting to waste a second of this rare opportunity.

Tattoo on one of his biceps? Check. Although his was in a stylized form of a dragon, much different than the more jagged, patterned version of the British dragon examples in the book.

After checking the section on tattoos, she looked up

again to see if his pupils flashed. When they didn't, back to the book she went.

Ah, they only flashed when the inner dragon talked to their human halves. Maybe the dragon was being quiet.

Just as she finished reading that, she glanced up and gasped.

Somehow, the dragonman had appeared right in front of her without her noticing. And if seeing his sexy, muscled form wasn't a big enough shock, his pupils flashed to slits and back.

Up close, it was fascinating and a teeny bit terrifying.

The dragonman grunted. "You. I want you."

She blinked. "M-Me?"

The ADDA employee stood next to him and raised her brows. "Are you backing out?"

For the briefest of seconds, Victoria considered it. The selected woman was to be whisked off to have lots and lots of sex with the dragonman, until she finally conceived his child.

And then, once the baby was born, she could either stay with the dragons or go back to her old life.

Could she do all of that, considering she'd never imagined she'd be chosen? Meaning she'd never mentally prepared to live with a large group of strangers.

The thought of strangers should make her sweat and it harder to breathe. But somewhere in her mind, she remembered they would all be *dragon-shifters*, meaning she would so many to watch and study.

The dragonman put out his hand. "Come with me."

His voice cut through her musings and she gazed into his dark brown eyes. Something about them, including the flashing pupils, reminded her that she'd always dreamed of a situation like this. And for once, she wasn't going to let her shyness steal an adventure from her.

If nothing else, the coming months would give her enough adventure for a lifetime. Then she could go back to her books and daydreaming about fantasy worlds and characters without regret.

As if someone else were controlling her body, Victoria snatched up her backpack and placed one hand in his. The warmth of his hands alone made her belly flutter. What would happen when he finally touched her naked body?

Trying not to blush, she was about to get up when he easily tugged her to her feet, the force enough to make her bump against his front.

His hard, hot front.

Trying not to gulp, she met his gaze again, only to find his pupils flashing rapidly, much quicker than before. She itched to consult the book again and see if it said what the action meant.

Then she remembered how if she went with him, she could ask as many questions as she liked. That gave her confidence a small kick.

He tugged her toward the rear exit. Victoria was vaguely aware of the ADDA employee following as someone began speaking up front.

However, Victoria didn't hear a word above her pounding heart. His grip was firm and slightly rough, and simply the feel of his skin against hers was one of the most erotic things of her life.

She couldn't imagine what he'd do with those hands if she signed the paperwork. He'd strip her clothes, stroke her body, and maybe even make her orgasm with just his fingers.

And while all of that made her skin hot and clothes feel too tight, still her brain wouldn't let go of the fact she was the one going with him. He'd picked *her*. Out of everyone else in the room.

Maybe she should stay quiet, but she blurted, "Why me?"

The dragon-shifter's dark brown eyes met hers and he stated, "Because you intrigue me."

She resisted shivering at his deep voice.

He didn't say another word, merely guiding her down the corridor, to another, smaller room. Inside were some refreshments, a small sofa, and a table piled with papers and binders, chairs on either side of it.

The ADDA employee motioned toward each of them as she said, "The first step is to talk a little and go over the agreements and rules together. Jose will let me know when you're done. Take as much time as you need, but no more than two hours. We have a schedule to follow." She held out a smartphone to Victoria. "My number is the only one in there right now. Call me if you need me to come back, Ms..." She glanced at her name tag and back. "Ms. Lewis."

Taking the phone, Victoria nodded. After the ADDA employee gave the dragon-shifter a long look, she left.

The room fell silent, although her heart was beating so hard that she wondered if the dragoman could hear it. After all, dragon-shifters had keener senses than humans.

As the seconds ticked by, Victoria wished she could be one of those people who could make witty remarks to break the silence.

But she wasn't one. So instead, she smiled and said, "Nice to meet you."

Chapter Two

As the human said, "Nice to meet you," Jose resisted laughing. He knew one of the other dragonmen from another clan in the greater Tahoe area who'd participated in the lottery a few years ago. And according to him, the female had purred and thrown herself at him at the first opportunity.

This...Victoria Lewis...didn't look to be about ready to throw herself at him at all.

Which intrigued him all the more.

His dragon bobbed his head. *And that's a good thing. After all, we want more from our true mate.*

Are you absolutely sure, dragon? She's pretty, and I'll have no trouble kissing her and getting it up, but she's not what I imagined she'd be.

No, she's not a dragon-shifter. But usually these things work out well in the end.

Usually being the operative word. When true mates went wrong, it usually went drastically wrong.

His dragon growled. *That won't happen to us as long as you be nice and try to woo her.*

Ignoring his beast, Jose released her hand and decided he may as well get things started. The sooner everything was signed, the sooner he could get the human alone and talk her into his bed.

And yes, as he glanced down at her small breasts, flaring hips, and curvy thighs made to lock around his head as he ate her pussy until she screamed, he very much wanted to do that, true mate or not.

His dragon growled. *Not before telling her the full truth.*

The truth meant explaining how kissing a true mate on the mouth would kick off a mate-claim frenzy, which was a nonstop sex marathon until she ended up pregnant. *We'll see.*

You can't keep it from her. She'll get scared and run when she can.

Jose had heard stories of such things happening, but this was different. *If she signs the contract, she can't leave.*

Is that really how you want things to start with her? Because she could leave later.

And while his inner beast didn't say the rest, Jose knew it—his dragon could go rogue if they claimed their true mate and she ran. And if he shifted and became uncontrollable, it was possible **ADDA** would hunt him down and kill him.

He replied, *I won't let it happen. I have a plan, so just bear with me.*

The human's brows drew together and she blurted, "Is your dragon talking to you? That's what your flashing pupils are about, right?" She didn't wait for him to answer, but pushed on. "Then what does he talk about? I've always been curious."

If I took control, then I would tell her, his dragon muttered.

Ignoring his beast, he answered the human. "Yes, he talks a lot. Too much sometimes. But as for what he's saying right now, that'll have to wait. I can't divulge dragon-shifter secrets after all, at least not until the contracts are signed."

She raised the book she'd been reading. "Unless you're a completely different species from the British dragons, then I don't see what great secrets you could still have."

He leaned down and murmured, "I've met my fair share of humans, but I'd bet a million bucks that you have a few secrets of your own, don't you? Maybe ones you only let come out at night, in your dreams?"

Her cheeks flushed, and the sight made his heart rate kick up. She'd been pretty before, but now she was fucking gorgeous. Jose wondered if her entire body would flush as he thrust between her thighs, making her come harder than she ever had before.

She cleared her throat. "Of course I have secrets, but not about being human. You could learn anything you wanted about us from a textbook. There aren't as many factual books about dragon-shifters, though. And I prefer facts over scary stories used to frighten children at bedtime."

Did her tone seem…disappointed? And why did he have the urge to tell her whatever she wanted, so she'd lean forward and hang on his every word?

His dragon stated, *You know why.*

Not wanting to think about how a true mate could have such sway over him, he motioned toward the table. "You'll learn more about my kind simply from the paperwork. Let's get started." He searched her gaze. "Unless you want to run away?"

She stood a fraction taller and clutched the book against her chest. While she was trying for brave, the backpack hanging from one shoulder sort of negated the image.

And for whatever reason, Jose found the sight adorable.

What the hell? He didn't find anything fucking adorable.

Damn true mate and her ability to make him even think of the word.

Victoria walked to the table to lay down her book, tossed her bag on the floor, and went to the refreshment table. As she piled cookies and chips on her plate, he watched how she picked things out carefully. No grabbing and moving on for her. No, she considered every piece and then made the decision.

Maybe she'd be as thorough with his body, learning every inch before finally taking his cock into her mouth.

His dragon snorted. *That's not how babies are made, which means she doesn't have to do that if she chooses.*

Oh, I think she'll want it eventually. Sometimes the quieter ones are the most adventurous in bed.

Says who?

Everybody.

She finally filled up her plate and selected a bottle of ice tea before sliding into one of the chairs at the table.

Not bothering with food, he sat across from her, making sure his leg "accidentally" brushed against hers. The human had the cookie midway to her mouth and froze. He tried rubbing his leg against hers, and she met his gaze.

The heat and curiosity there made his cock instantly hard.

Ah, yes, he was going to enjoy this human in his bed.

He just needed to get her to sign the fucking paperwork first.

Opening one of the binders, he gave it to her and took another. Even if this was boring, and not what he wanted to do right now, he would make it a game. How much coaxing under the table would it take to make her touch him back?

The dragon in him settled down with wide eyes. Dragons liked games, and Victoria Lewis had just become the most exciting one of their lives.

As the dragonman's leg brushed against hers, she froze. Not out of fear, but each small rub of his jean-clad leg against her own made her belly flip and heat rush between her thighs.

She knew the purpose of all this was sex and a baby, but did he really want her so badly that he'd resort to nearly playing footsie under the table?

Then his leg moved between hers, gently nudging them apart.

And for a second, she thought if she only moved forward a little on her seat, his knee could reach the currently throbbing bundle of nerves there.

However, Jose removed his leg and sat back in his chair, a smug look on his face. "Are you going to eat that or not?"

Glancing at the forgotten cookie in her hand, she resisted scowling. He damn well knew why she'd forgotten about it. It wasn't every day a hot, sexy dragonman tried to get between your legs.

She should toss it down and then look at the first page of the binder. However, somewhere deep inside, in that place she usually reserved for fantasies and dreams, an idea burst forth. Never tearing her gaze away, she licked the edge of the cookies slowly, flicking her tongue against the edge a few times before bringing it to her lips. After running it slowly back and forth, she finally took a bite.

And she heard the dragonman suck in a breath.

Triumph coursed through her body. For the first time in her life, she'd been able to be as smooth as in her fantasies.

However, the happiness didn't last long because Jose took the cookie from her hands, popped the rest into his mouth, and moved her plate away. "I see you're hungry, human. If you want a taste of what you're really dying to lick, then let's get started."

With two sentences, her cheeks burned. So much for being smooth and sexy, acting as if she taunted dragon-shifters any day of the week.

Picking up the binder, she did her best to focus on the front page. What she found made her frown.

SUMMARY

Before going any further, you agree to sexually be at the mercy of one dragon-shifter for as long as it takes to conceive. Dragon-shifters are fierce in bed, and if this scares you, call the ADDA employee to leave now. You've been warned.

WHOA. They weren't holding anything back, were they?

And that inner piece of herself couldn't help but murmur, "Methinks dragons overstate their abilities."

Jose's leg was back between hers, his knees nearly touching her center. He said, "I'll have to try harder than before to prove it's true, won't I?"

Looking up, she gasped at the heat in his eyes. Add in the flashing pupils, and it was clear she wasn't around an ordinary, cocky human man.

This was a dragon-shifter, and one who apparently liked to prove things.

Maybe that wouldn't be so bad after all.

Glad she didn't say it aloud—she'd only get more embarrassed—she cleared her throat for what felt like the hundredth time that day. "I'm sure you're adequate."

His leg moved closer, his knee grazing her clit and making her gasp before he retreated. Pleasure rushed through her body, drenching her panties and it took everything she had not to ask him to do it again.

He smiled slowly. "You know dragon-shifters have keen senses, so I know you're eager for me to prove it, too."

He could *smell* her.

Maybe that would turn off some women, but it only made her wetter.

Which made it harder to concentrate. So she pulled back and scooted further down the table, out of the reach of his knee. "You won't be able to prove anything if we don't get through this. So, let's get started."

As she started to read, Jose crossed his arms over his chest and merely watched her. After a few minutes, she peeked up. "Aren't you going to read it, too?"

"I already did. And I have an eidetic memory, so I remember every word."

Of course, the sexy as hell, muscled man who could

change into a damn *dragon* also had an eidetic memory. "Are you immortal, too, while you're at it?"

He snorted. "No, but I'm sure someone is working on that."

And he had a sense of humor.

If she stayed around him long enough, would she be able to just leave him at the end of all this?

Or would he want her to stay with him?

Stop with the romance novel-line of thinking, Tori. He wanted a conquest, not a wife. That wasn't a requirement of this whole thing.

So she went back to reading, signing when needed, and reminded herself this was about sex, getting pregnant, and nothing more.

As long as she remembered that, her heart would remain in one piece.

Maybe.

Chapter Three

A couple of hours later, Jose tapped his fingers against his thigh and wished the ADDA employee would drive a little faster.

The sooner they arrived at the cabin, the sooner he could strip the human and carry out his promise.

Damn, she'd been flirting and sexier than any female he'd ever met, all while filling out fucking paperwork.

His dragon spoke up. *Then tell her we're her true mate. She deserves to know.*

Eventually. I want to tease her sweet cunt first, make her scream, and then tell her.

Why? Are you afraid she'll say no and ask to leave?

It really shouldn't matter what Victoria would do, but Jose desperately wanted her to stay.

No female had ever been so easy to talk to, not even among his own kind. Yes, she found him hot and wanted him between her thighs as soon as possible, but there was more than wanting to bag him and run away. She was curious, and that might be enough to convince her of more.

Maybe, just maybe, fate had been right about this. Maybe she was his one female to hold, protect, and treasure above all else.

His dragon snorted. *Since when are you romantic?*

Fuck if I know. The female does strange things to me.

And she didn't even have to be next to him, or across from him, to do so.

Victoria was being driven in a separate car, to give her one last chance to ask questions, or even back out with only a minor penalty this early in the game.

Jose dug his nails into his thigh. She'd better not run away. Even if it was against the terms of the agreement, he would try chasing after her.

He wanted to growl but didn't want to alarm Ashley. So he went back to tapping his fingers and remembering his little human licking that cookie, showing him what she'd do with his cock.

A cock that hadn't stopped being hard since he'd first been alone with her.

Ashley snorted from the driver's side. "For someone who was so reluctant not a few hours ago, you're all but bursting to get there and be with her, aren't you?"

He looked at her askance. "Isn't that a good thing?"

After a beat, Ashley asked, "Is she your true mate? If so, you should tell her. I've been working with ADDA for nearly ten years, and if you want any chance of a future with a human, you have to tell her."

"I will."

Ashly tapped the steering wheel. "So she is, then. That's only the second time that's happened from the lotteries, that I recall."

He knew that and had rather hoped his sister would be the one to find her true mate, not him.

But now he'd seen and talked with Victoria, there was no fucking way he was going to let her go.

They finally arrived at the outer gates of the cabin— or, rather, he thought of it as a small compound—and were let inside a minute later. When Ashely finally pulled in front of the large, rustic-looking building and turned off the engine, she turned partway toward him. "I mean it, tell her before you kiss her. Otherwise, you could face the worst kind of hell. She could choose to remain on PineRock with the child and pick another dragonman to act as the father. And you could do nothing about it."

He grunted. "I get it, okay? It may be hard to believe, but most of the time, we function perfectly well without the American Department of Dragon Affairs telling us what to do. I don't need babying."

"Maybe not, but I'm just trying to be nice here. I've seen a dragonman whose true mate refused him, and he's still in pure hell, five years later. Even though I wouldn't say I love your sparkling personality, I wouldn't wish that on anyone."

Jose knew who she was talking about, everyone in

PineRock did. Cole lived in near isolation, taking every fucking risk he could with the rescue teams and fire-fighters in the area, almost as if he were hoping fate would kill him and end his misery.

"I know." He paused and muttered, "Thank you."

"See, that wasn't so hard, was it? You were nice and didn't even burst into flames."

Rolling his eyes, he opened the door. "I'm leaving now."

"And I'll be counting down the days until the frenzy is over. Maybe I'll even get my fiancé to bake you a super cute cake to celebrate fatherhood, one filled with adorable baby tokens and lots of flowers. Pink ones that sparkle? Right?"

Flipping her the bird, he slammed the door and entered the cabin. He had another five or ten minutes before Victoria arrived.

If she arrived.

His beast growled. *She'll be here.*

Since he thought so, too, Jose went to work getting everything ready. He wasn't going to waste time once his human arrived. And even if he could be a surly bastard, Jose knew a little seduction never hurt.

And so he went to work.

VICTORIA STOOD in front of the cabin, her jaw dropped,

trying to even rationalize how anyone would call it such a thing.

The house was rustic, looking like a log cabin, but it was three-stories tall and bigger than the house she'd grown up in. Hell, bigger than any house on her entire street.

Did they provide a house this size so that they had room to ignore each other if they started to get on one another's nerves? Otherwise, she couldn't imagine why it wouldn't be a small cabin. It'd be cozy and romantic. The perfect place to get to know the dragonman.

Then she remembered that romance wasn't a requirement of the deal.

The ADDA employee who'd driven her to the cabin honked her horn, reminding Victoria that she wouldn't leave until she was inside.

Even though she had every right to enter, she knocked. A second later, Jose opened the door.

And the man was shirtless.

As she gaped at the chiseled muscles of his chest and abs, she forgot all about the house, the employee, and even how chilly it was. She'd always thought the information about how dragon-shifters were so toned from all the flying in their dragon form had to be an exaggeration.

Apparently not.

Her gaze dipped lower, to the trail of hair going down his abdomen and she bit her lip at the erection punching against his jeans.

A rather sizable one.

With a growl, Jose pulled her inside and shut the door. In the next beat, she was pinned against it, his face mere inches from hers.

As his hot breath danced across her lips, a barely there caress, her knees nearly gave out. She was finally alone with him, the sexy dragon-shifter with an eidetic memory. The one who probably would've given her an orgasm earlier, in the small meeting room, if she'd allowed it.

What would he do now, she wondered, anticipation making her heart pound.

Careful, Tori. Don't get in over your head.

Jose murmured, "Didn't your book tell you to be careful when dealing with a horny dragon-shifter?"

"N-Not much. Just that you need to be really sure you want it before being alone with one."

He traced her cheek, then her mouth, tracing the shape of each lip. As he gently stroked back and forth across her bottom lip, the touch made her nipples and center throb. Her mouth opened slightly as if trying to gasp.

At this rate, she wouldn't have a chance to ask him any questions before they were both naked and "getting to work" as Ashley had put it.

As Jose spoke, Victoria somehow managed to hear his words despite his steady caress against her mouth. "Yes, wanting it—hot, sweaty, life-changing sex—is true." He pressed the very tip of his forefinger inside her mouth, but he removed the digit before she could nibble it.

Nibble it? Yes, bookworm extraordinaire Victoria Lewis had been about to lightly bite a dragonman's finger.

His pupils flashed before he murmured, "And since you're here, that must mean you're really sure about what comes next."

She nodded, wishing she had some sort of witty remark to make. But Victoria surprised even herself when she asked, "When do we get started?"

He groaned before lowering his head to her earlobe. He nipped it before licking the sting, and she leaned more heavily against the door. A part of her wished he'd shred her clothes with his talons—she was pretty sure they could change only part of their bodies like that— hoist her up and fuck her against the door. Hard.

What? She had no idea where that thought had come from. Maybe he emitted some sort of pheromone that acted as an aphrodisiac.

After nipping her ear again, he said, "I know what my little human needs. But to make extra sure, strip and sit on the couch."

His request made her cheeks burn. Never had she stripped for a man before, let alone on the day she'd just met him. "Can't I go to the bathroom first to freshen up?" *And build up my courage.*

He kissed her jaw. "No way. I burn to see your lovely skin, human." His voice lowered a fraction. "And I don't want to wait to see just how wet and swollen you are for me already."

Damn, at his dirty words, her clit throbbed as she nearly lifted her hips against him. *Okay.* She could do this. "Then you're going to have to step back. I don't have superhuman strength like you, unless you want me to knee you in the balls to get free?"

"You don't want to do that, human." His hand lightly brushed her side, his touch leaving electricity in its wake before he stepped back. "Otherwise, you'd have to wait for me to bury myself deep inside your tight pussy, deeper than you've ever felt before, and I don't think you want to wait, either."

Her breasts grew even heavier, and she burned to strip and let him do what he wanted.

Never had she felt this at ease with a man, let alone this soon.

Maybe he had super dragon-shifter powers of seduction.

Jose moved to stand near the couch and he raised an eyebrow in question.

I guess that means it's time to try and strip for a dragonman.

She took a deep breath and tossed her backpack into a chair. And even though her cheeks still burned, she couldn't tear her gaze away from Jose's, his eyes flashing and full of heat.

No man had ever looked at her like that, as if she were the most desirable woman in the world.

It would be easy to get used to that look.

No. No thoughts of the future. Raising her chin a fraction, Victoria took a few steps closer to the couch, debating when to try and strip for him. Not that she was an expert in any way. But, hell, if this was going to be the biggest adventure of her life, she was going to start doing her best to make it a good one.

Even if she ended up with her hair getting stuck on a button and she had to hop and ask for help to get free, which would be just her luck.

That would most definitely not be what the dragonman expected.

Biting her lip to keep from laughing at his imagined reaction, she unzipped her jacket slowly, loving how Jose's eyes followed the movement. As she tugged the sleeve off, she puffed out her chest and leaned forward a little, ensuring he could see down her shirt.

And yes, he stared down her shirt, his eyes flashing as he growled.

Her heart pounded so hard it was all she could hear. But still, she tossed the jacket aside and reached for the hem of her top. Slowly she brought it up, making sure to rub it a few times over her aching nipples, and moaned without thought.

Jose ran a hand over his mouth as he murmured, "Fuck, now I'm jealous of a shirt."

His words boosted her confidence, and she tugged the top all the way off—carefully avoiding the decorative enemy buttons—and tossed it at him.

He caught it, bringing it to his nose, and inhaling deeply. His pupils remained slitted longer than she'd seen since meeting him, eventually becoming round again.

He reached out a hand, then pulled it back. "Keep going, human. If you stop again, I'll shred the rest of your clothes off with one talon."

So she'd been right—he could change a nail to a talon only.

Then it hit her—the man could shift into a who-knew-how-many-feet-tall dragon. One she didn't even know the color of. And for some reason, she needed to know something, anything, about him to make this seem more real.

Jose took a step toward her, and she blurted, "What color is your dragon?"

He blinked, clearly not expecting the question. He answered, "Blue."

"Will I ever see him?"

"That depends on whether you finish stripping right this second or not."

She tried to muster up the courage she'd had a few seconds ago, and failed. It seemed her boldness had been temporary, which made sense, given that she usually wasn't that way.

He closed the distance between them. But instead of ripping off her clothes, he put a finger under her chin and forced her to meet his gaze—a searing look, filled with desire. "What's wrong?"

Now he was surprising her. Patience wasn't usually at the top of the list of traits she had for dragon-shifters.

With anyone else, she probably would've looked away and said nothing and tried to change the subject.

However, as Jose stroked the underside of her chin, the words simply flew from her lips. "I know so little about you and yet I'm about to have sex with you. It's kind of weird."

One corner of his mouth kicked up. "You must not be the one-night-stand type of human female, right?"

He had no idea. "Honestly? I didn't think you'd pick me back at the hotel. And I think the more we interact, the more the shock and excitement fades, allowing reality to set in." She paused a beat before forcing out the rest, "And that makes me a little nervous."

Leaning closer, Jose asked, "Did you change your mind?"

As she stared into his eyes, a deep brown filled with curiosity, she thought about it. But "no" screamed through her mind. She'd put her name into the lottery on a whim and had accepted her place in order to learn as much as possible, and nothing more.

But now that he'd touched her skin, nibbled her earlobe, and made her the most turned on in her life, she couldn't go back to only wanting to study him.

No, she wanted to get to know him better, in all ways. Because there was no way she was going to wonder "what if" for the rest of her life. "No, I didn't change my mind. But maybe we could slow it down a little? You haven't even kissed me yet."

His pupils flashed, but she couldn't read his expression.

What she wouldn't give to be able to talk to his inner dragon.

Slowly Jose moved his head to her cheek, kissed her once—his firm, warm lips making her shiver—and then whispered, "There, you've been kissed."

She surprised herself by growling. "That's not what I meant."

One of his hands touched her hip, then slowly moved to her belly before sliding lower to cup her and rock the heel of his hand against her clit. Victoria sucked in a breath as he spoke again. "How about I kiss you here?"

Oh how she wanted to scream yes and shuck her pants. Many a novel showed the woman receiving mind-blowing oral sex, but Victoria had yet to find a real-life man who knew what he was doing down there.

She snorted at the image of Jose fumbling around. She just couldn't picture it.

After all, the dragonman seemed to be so very good at everything else. She couldn't imagine his pride, let alone his dragon, failing at that, too.

Jose met her gaze again. "What's so funny?"

Shaking her head, she answered, "No, I can't tell you. It's embarrassing."

Removing his hand from between her legs, he took her face between both of his. "Nothing should be too embarrassing between us. Ever."

The surety of his tone, along with something that must be the dominance dragon-shifters threaded into their voices—she'd read about it in the book—made her believe him. "I'm eventually a sure thing, so there's no need to butter me up."

His eyes flashed again and his low growl made her shiver—in a good way. "I'm not trying to talk you up. It's the truth—don't hold back from me, Victoria. Ever."

She stopped breathing a second at the intensity of his words.

He meant them.

And now Victoria was starting to think dragon-shifter men were too good to be true.

Without thought, she replied, "Tori. My friends and family call me Tori."

"Tori," he murmured. "Yes, I think that suits you better."

She raised her brows. "How can you say that? You don't even know me."

He grinned. "I know you like to strip, and don't hold back when I have my hands between your legs. You rocked against my palm without thought, as you should." He strummed his thumbs against her cheeks. "That's something Tori would do, not a Victoria."

She tentatively reached a hand out to his chest, feeling his taut muscles beneath her fingers. Mustering her courage again, she asked, "And what would a Jose do in this situation?"

His pupils turned to slits for a few beats before returning to normal. "How about I show you?"

Her heart thundered inside her chest. If she were a

betting woman, she'd say he wanted her naked so he could do naughty things to her.

But could she do it? Let a man she'd just met have free reign of her body just like that?

As he continued to caress her cheeks, she thought yes, yes she could. She nodded. "Okay."

Without a word, he scooped her up as if she weighed nothing. She squeaked. "What are you doing?"

His eyes turned predatory. "Showing you what Jose would do."

Maybe she should protest, but she merely looped her hands behind his neck and stared into his eyes. The way they flashed fascinated her. "Do your eyes sometimes stay slitted for long periods?"

He grunted. "At times."

Judging by the way he tensed under her body, she sensed he was hiding something.

But before she could voice her thoughts, Jose stopped in front of the sofa and lowered her down to her feet slowly, so that her body felt every inch of his torso, until his erection pressed against her belly.

Neither of them moved, gazing into each other's eyes, as heat and wanting spread through Victoria's body.

And just by how hard he was, through Jose's, too.

Finally he moved back a few inches and his hands went to the button of her jeans. He paused a beat, no doubt giving her time to tell him to stop, but she gripped his bicep and squeezed in encouragement. The action kicked him into gear, and he had her jeans unzipped and off faster than she'd thought possible, especially since he had to take off her shoes, too.

Victoria stood, only in her bra and panties, in front of the sexiest man she'd ever seen. A dragonman who looked at her as if she were the plumpest, juiciest steak, ready for him to eat and devour with relish.

His fingers went to the band of her underwear, a talon lightly brushed against her skin. She drew in a breath, and he growled. "Someday, I will shred these off your body. But right now, we'll keep them whole until your clothes arrive."

She wanted to scream for him to shred them, but he tugged them down inch by agonizing inch, the slight friction of the fabric against her skin making her body temperature skyrocket.

Just what did he do to her?

She finally stepped out of them and moved to take off her bra, but he stilled her hand. "Not yet. I don't want to risk the distraction."

"Distraction? From what?"

He pressed her to sit on the couch before spreading her thighs. As he stared between her legs, her face burned as she gleamed his answer.

Then Jose licked his lips, and her center pounded, aching to feel the pressure of his tongue.

He groaned. "I can smell how sweet you are. I think it's about time to taste you."

As he knelt before her, Victoria dug her nails into the cushions of the couch.

It looked like her newfound adventure was quickly turning into one of the many fantasies she'd created over the years.

And she only hoped he lived up to it. Because if anyone could, she sensed it was the dragonman kneeling before her.

Chapter Four

Not immediately throwing his female down and making her come with his tongue was one of the hardest things Jose had resisted in a while.

But she had seemed unsure after the fucking amazing strip she'd done—even if it'd only been removing her jacket and shirt—and he hated the change of her confidence level.

Removing the remainder of her clothes had washed most of the anxiety away, to the point his inner dragon growled, *Tell her the truth. She should know she's our true mate.*

Soon, but not yet.

No, he needed to ensure she was as relaxed as possible before he told her what could happen after he kissed her sweet mouth.

Luckily, he knew what to do and it meant learning one of the things he burned to know about her—the taste of her sweet honey.

So Jose knelt between her legs and stared at her wet, swollen center, already glistening for him. Not to mention her scent was stronger now and damn, she smelled better than anything he'd scented before, which only made his mouth water in anticipation.

After stroking the silky skin of her inner thighs a few times, the final wisps of tension faded from her muscles, letting him know she was ready. With a growl, he leaned down and blew up her slit and back down.

Victoria sucked in a breath, her nails digging even harder into the cushions, and he smiled. She probably wanted to grab his head and guide him down, but held back. He suspected his human wanted him dirty, their sex as well, but was shy to admit it.

That just added another level of complexity to the prize that was Victoria Lewis.

Jose finally closed the distance and gave one slow, long lick up her slit, just stopping short of her bundle of nerves at the top. She moaned, but he barely heard it as he went for another lick, and another, wanting to brand her sweet and salty taste into his memory.

Keeping her hips in place, he lightly fucked her opening with his tongue, plunging, tickling, teasing her until she was all but ripping the material of the couch with her nails. If she didn't touch him soon, he'd make her.

Focusing on his female's sweet center, he licked up slowly, this time up toward her clit, but only circled it without quite touching it.

His female moved her hips, trying to get his tongue where she wanted it.

And yet, he wanted her to demand it. So Jose continued his torture, licking up and around, never quite touching, his cock aching with each sip of her taste.

Victoria finally put a hand on his head, threading her fingers through his hair. *Yes,* both man and beast screamed. *Dig your nails in and demand that I make you come.*

When she didn't, he increased his nips, licks, and tongue fucking until she finally pressed his head toward her, her nails lightly scratching his scalp.

Yes. One day, his mate would tell him exactly what she needed so he could give it to her.

Wanting to reward her, he flicked her tight bud once. Her throaty scream made his cock pulse and let out a drop of moisture.

She put her other hand on his head and pressed harder. Taking the cue, he suckled her hard clit between his lips and stroked with his tongue. She pressed her hips upward, but he kept her in place, resisting the urge to fuck her with his fingers at the same time.

He was only going to use his mouth to make her scream the first time.

Jose let her clit go and continued to lap her pussy before heading back up and twirling her tight bud. He bit down hard, and Victoria dug her nails into his scalp.

Well, well, his female liked it a little rough.

He did it again, and she bucked upward, moaning as she came. He quickly moved his tongue to lap her pussy, reveling in her taste and slowing spasms, growling even harder when he could taste her orgasm.

When she finally lay back against the couch, spent, he licked up her slit one more time before raising his head. Victoria's eyes were half-lidded, her face and entire upper body flushed.

The sight of his female sated made him only want to do it again.

He kissed up her body, between her breast, and finally to her jaw. "Well?"

"I-I don't know what to say."

He chuckled as he watched for her reaction. "Maybe something along the lines that was the best tongue fucking of my life?"

Her blush deepened and she bit that delectable lower lip again. She was going to make them plump without him ever touching them.

His beast whispered, *I don't want to wait. Tell her. Now. Soon. She's almost ready.*

She raised a hand and lightly touched his jaw. Surprising even himself, he leaned into her caress.

Never had a female been so gentle with him. And he craved more of it. Much more.

She finally spoke, her voice a bit husky. "You've proven the myth of great oral sex can be a reality."

The thought of her never receiving the worship she was due made him want to punch something.

However, he didn't want to bring her past lovers into this. They were bastards, all of them. From now on, she'd have him and only him. And soon those memories would fade for good.

He threaded his fingers through hers and leaned forward. "With a dragon-shifter, that was merely the beginning. We take our female's pleasure seriously. If I don't make you come, then I shouldn't, either."

She tilted her head, making her dark hair fall over one shoulder.

Even with her half-naked and smelling of sex, he wanted to lean over and rub his cheek against her soft tresses.

Damn, the romantic shit kept coming to him now.

Shaking her head, Victoria replied, "I'm not sure I believe that. It sounds like something from a book."

She kept talking about books, his human. Although, given her recent comments, it made him curious as to just what she was reading.

He rubbed her legs, loving how she unconsciously parted them further in invitation, turning his dick to granite.

His dragon roared. *How can you resist her? She's right there, our true mate. Tell her and kiss her.*

Ignoring his dragon—although it was getting harder to do and a line he'd need to tread carefully—he focused on his female. He replied, "Oh, you'll learn what I say is the truth soon enough, my sweet Tori." He moved until his face was an inch from hers. "Because I'm never going to let you go."

She lifted one shoulder. "Again, I'm a sure thing, so no need to talk me up."

He growled. "I'm not trying to butter you up. You're mine, Victoria Lewis. Forever."

Whether his human was ready for the news or not, it was time to tell her the truth about what would happen once he kissed her sweet lips.

EVEN VICTORIA's post-orgasmic hazed brain caught the finality of his tone. "What do you mean, forever?"

Tightening his fingers around hers, he murmured, "You're my true mate, Tori. Do you know what that means?"

Her first reaction was to consult her book. But even without it, she knew the basics—each dragon-shifter had a fated true mate. That person was their best chance at happiness.

Although she couldn't remember the rest of the details. And thankfully, she was still boneless from her orgasm, or no doubt she'd be freaking out a little. "I'm your true mate? How is that possible? I'm human."

He smiled. "It doesn't matter. Dragon-shifters mate humans, even the author of the book you hold so dear mated one."

True. The author, Melanie Hall-MacLeod, a human, had mated a famously sexy, growly dragonman of her own.

Still, as the truth began to sink in, she tried to focus on her trusted, long-time friend—facts. "How do you even know it's me? You just met me a few hours ago. I'm not sure I accept the 'one look and done' theory, either."

"An inner male dragon senses their true mate. And while there may be dragons who lie about it if they're spoiled and selfish, mine would never do so." He tried to soften his face a fraction as he took her hands in his and he continued, "Besides, look at how far we've come already. It's almost as if your body understands that you're mine."

His words reminded her that she was naked from the waist down and a few minutes ago, the very large drag-onman had been licking between her thighs as if he'd never get enough.

Willing her cheeks not to burn—the talk of true mates was a serious thing—she blurted, "That's unhelp-ful. You're sexy, so of course I'm going to act like a wanton with you between my thighs." She sat up a little taller, hoping Jose would remove himself from between her legs, but he didn't budge.

As she searched his gaze and flashing pupils, she wondered if it could be true. That somehow, someway, this man's inner dragon had taken one look at her and said, "*Mine.*"

The side of her full of daydreams and fantasies wanted to accept the idea and kiss the man to get their new life started. However, her more rational side won out for the moment, and she said, "If you're being serious, then I need more information. What does being a true mate fully mean, because I don't know. Plus—do I even have a choice in the matter? Or will ADDA simply force me to stay with the dragons, to help keep the peace?"

While she was interested in dragons, not to mention Jose was also sexy and somewhat charming, was that enough to throw caution to the wind and seize an unknown future? One maybe where she couldn't decide anything ever again?

She tried to pull her hands away, but he didn't let go. Jose never broke his gaze as he said, "There's no need to be afraid. It's not a future of you being a sex slave in a dungeon, Tori. Let me explain it first, then you can make a decision, okay?" She bobbed her head and he grunted. "Good, then let's try this as I do that."

He moved to sit on the couch and pulled her into his lap, his hot chest against her bicep, the contact making her relax her posture a little.

Even though his arms were wrapped around her, keeping her in his lap, she was a little less vulnerable and able to think clearer.

"Better?" he murmured.

"A little."

His pupils flashed again, but quickly returned to round and stayed that way, which made her heart calm a fraction.

Not that she wasn't interested in his dragon, but right now, she needed the human half to explain everything.

After squeezing her waist in reassurance, Jose continued, "As I said, my inner dragon recognizes you as my true mate, which means it's the truth. I didn't say anything at first because I wanted to show you how good it can be between us, even without fate."

She shook her head. "One orgasm a secure future does not make."

"No. But answer me this—has it ever felt so easy, so right with another male this quickly?"

She could lie, but it wasn't as if she made a convincing liar anyway. "No."

"Exactly. It's because you've always been meant to be mine. And no, not as a mere possession, but my partner in all things. One with as much free will as any dragon-shifter has under ADDA, at least. Although I can't force you to stay with me always. It will be your choice."

If she did, it meant ADDA would place a lot of new restrictions on her if she agreed to stick around. Ones that would mostly keep her from her friends and family.

Before her mind whirred with all the possible changes, Jose moved a hand to her lower back and rubbed it in slow circles. The longer he did it, the less nervous she felt.

Seriously, dragon-shifters must have some sort of powers of seduction or something.

Giving herself a mental shake, she focused on the possibly life-changing situation at hand. "Say I accept your claim that I'm your true mate. What happens next, step-by-step? And before you tease me, I hadn't really memorized everything in that section of the book since I didn't think I'd be hanging out one-on-one with dragon-shifters any time soon."

He brushed a section of hair off her face. "You should've expected it to happen. Even in a room of a thousand females, a million, I would've noticed you above the rest."

His words made her relax a fraction. Maybe they were bullshit, but her gut said not.

True mates were serious things to dragon-shifters.

"Okay, so you noticed me and reassured me I won't be a sex slave. And if I stay, ADDA will put me under a bunch of new rules. But what else? I sense there's a part of it you haven't explained yet, something important."

His pupils flashed to slits and back—what was his dragon telling him?—before Jose finally answered, "The condensed version is this—I kiss you and it kicks off a mate-claim frenzy where we have sex until you're pregnant."

She resisted blinking. That was it? "So far, that was the aim of this anyway. So what else is there?"

For the first time since she'd met him, Jose hesitated a beat. But the expression vanished so quickly that Victoria doubted she'd seen it at all.

He said, "Once I kiss you, my inner dragon is bound to come out. Not in his dragon form, but rather he takes over my mind and controls my human body. However, dragons are more animalistic, possessive, and act on instinct. He may be rough. No, fuck that, I know he will. And that scares a lot of humans."

The fact the tall, imposing male worried she'd run because of his horny dragon half did something to her insides. Even knowing it could scare her, he was revealing it all to her.

And for the first time, she wondered if she could see a future with him. Oh, she still didn't know him well beyond the fact he knew how to make her orgasm, but she'd heard tales of how a dragon's true mate was rare, a blessing of sorts, and it could be the best thing to happen to someone.

Not necessarily a guarantee, but better odds than with anyone else.

She finally raised a hand to touch his cheek, loving his late-date stubble against her fingers, needing to touch him right now. "Then let me talk with your inner dragon. If I do it now before we kiss, then I won't be scared when he comes out in the frenzy."

Yep, it looked like she'd signed up for the frenzy already.

His pupils flashed right before he said, "If I let him out now, and he kisses you, he may be the first to claim you, not me. Is that something you could handle?"

She searched his gaze. "So, a stranger would just pin me down and have his way with me?"

He shook his head. "My dragon is part of me, not a stranger at all. Even if this half of me isn't in control, both halves make up one male named Jose."

She tried to wrap her head around it. "That seems just...weird."

He snorted. "It's not the easiest thing for humans to understand." His gaze turned heated. "But if you let me kiss you, then you're going to get a one-on-one crash course on how it all works."

As his fingers strummed the skin at her waist, she relaxed a fraction.

She could either have Jose kiss her now and then face his dragon when the time came, unsure of what to expect. Or, she could have his beast come out to show her what happens with the other half in control and then possibly have the dragon-possessed man kiss her and go all instinctual on her.

Could it be that bad, either way? The book on dragon-shifters had been lovingly dedicated to Melanie's dragonman and children. And the few video clips she'd seen of some of the other British dragon couples had shown just as a devoted pair.

Maybe, if she jumped, she'd fall right into the fantasy she'd always wanted.

Of course, she could also plunge too deep and suffer the consequences.

But as Jose's eyes continued to flash and his fingers brushed her skin, Victoria made her decision—it was time to jump. "I have one more question before I give my answer."

"What is it?"

"Will your dragon always be in control during the frenzy, or will you come out, too?"

A determined glint in his eyes flared. "Oh, I'll be

coming out. Even if I have to fucking battle my dragon inside my head and toss him into a mental prison—it's a temporary way to keep him contained inside my mind— I'll do it. I'll be damned if he is the only one to enjoy your luscious body."

Making a mental prison to contain his inner beast? There was so much for Victoria to learn.

But she pushed it aside. If everything went right, she'd have plenty of time later to ask anything she wanted. Right now, it was time to stop stalling. She'd signed up for this, and even though she had gotten more than she bargained for, she wasn't going to run.

She'd wanted an adventure, and it looked like she was going to get a much bigger one than she'd bargained for.

Victoria maneuvered to straddle his lap and looped her hands behind his neck. "Let your dragon out. I'd rather meet him at first than be surprised later."

She expected Jose to be thrilled, but he frowned. "That means the bastard will get you first."

Tilting her head, she asked, "But I thought you were one and the same?"

"We are, but we're also competitive as hell. And I don't like to lose."

She smiled. "That just made things more interesting. A competition between you two? Does that mean I'm the final judge?"

"Don't encourage him," he said with a grunt.

Laughing, she moved even closer to him, until her

bra-covered breasts brushed his hard chest. "Let him out so we can get this started."

He lightly caressed her lower back. "My brave human."

For a few beats, they stared into one another's eyes and Victoria stopped breathing. Jose's pupils kept flashing, but the look of hunger and wanting never vanished.

Somehow, someway, this dragonman wanted her, and only her. Badly.

It took everything she had not to start riding his pants-covered cock. This dragon-shifter was fast becoming an addiction.

His voice finally broke the spell. "Don't worry, I'll be back as soon as I can wrangle control away from him again, Tori," he murmured before his pupils slitted and stayed that way.

And she waited to see what happened.

Chapter Five

———————————

J ose had wanted to be the one to claim Victoria first. But when she asked for him to let his dragon out and get it over with, he couldn't deny her.

It was, after all, a smart plan. Deal with the dragon and then there wouldn't be any surprises.

However, as he let his dragon to the forefront of his mind, he still glowered and muttered to his dragon, *Don't be stingy.*

She wanted me, so she's going to get me. For a while.

Fucking dragon. Jose only hoped his beast was riling him up on purpose and not speaking the truth. Because if he was, Jose would have a mental battle on his hands soon enough.

His dragon threaded their hand through Victoria's hair and growled, "My human is pretty, and wet, and waiting. I want you, to kiss you, to fuck you, to claim you." He moved closer. "Now."

Victoria searched his gaze and one corner of her mouth ticked up. "So, you have no filter, then?"

The fact his human was amused made Jose relax a little. His dragon frowned. "No, that's a human trait. I want you now. Why hide it?" He pulled her head closer until their lips were a hairsbreadth away. "Say yes."

"Yes," she breathed.

His lips descended on Victoria's, and the instant they touched, a shot of pure lust and need coursed through Jose's body. This was their mate, their female, and they needed to claim her.

Not once, but over and over again, until she carried both their scent and their young.

His dragon growled and devoured Victoria's mouth, licking, sucking, and nipping as he went. And his human merely took it at first until she finally started to kiss them back.

Damn, her taste. Between her pussy and her mouth, Jose didn't think he'd ever find anything as sweet ever again.

His dragon moved their hand to between her thighs and stroked her clit. Victoria jumped, breaking the kiss. His dragon breathed, "You're wet and ready for me. I want to fuck and claim you now."

Thank hell Jose had made her come already. Under normal circumstances, he'd told the truth—dragon-shifter males always ensured their mate came first.

The only exception? In the throes of a frenzy, sometimes it was lost, especially if the dragon half was in charge.

Even then, she'd come soon after, once he orgasmed. One thing he'd forgotten to tell Victoria was that his semen would send her into the wildest, most intense orgasm of her life.

His dragon lifted Victoria and rearranged her so that she faced away from them, leaning over the back of the couch, her perfectly full ass in the air.

Jose wanted to take his time caressing her soft flesh, making her arch her back, and beg for his dick.

But his dragon wasn't thinking of anything but being inside her. After pushing her legs apart, his beast ordered, "Arch for me. Now."

And she did without hesitation, making Jose want her all the more.

Fuck, he was tempted to wrestle control from his dragon.

But then he remembered that this is what his true mate wanted, and so he'd let her have it.

His dragon positioned their cock at her entrance, and growled, "Mine. You're going to be mine, always, mine."

He thrust in and Victoria cried out—in pleasure, not pain.

She was so tight, so wet, so fucking perfect.

His dragon didn't waste time moving his hips, increasing his pace, making the couch move with the force of his thrusts.

This was their female. His beast needed to brand her, fill her and claim her as many times as possible.

As he'd thought, his dragon turned rougher, not bothering to make love but fucking their mate, moving his hips, making her feel him deeper than she'd ever known possible.

The human part of him worried it was too much. The reality of a dragon half taking their mate was usually different than what a human could imagine.

But then Victoria reached back, her nails digging into his wrists, and she moaned. "Harder."

His beast roared, held her hips in place, and complied. The sound of flesh hitting flesh filled the room as each movement brought him closer to coming.

Then his dragon let go, stilled, and spent inside her. A beat later, Victoria followed, her cunt greedily milking him for his seed.

The pleasure was so intense Jose nearly forgot where he was, coming harder than he'd ever done before, losing all thought and possibly his damn mind.

Nothing compared to being inside his mate when it happened. Nothing.

She was his now, and neither man nor beast was going to let her go. Ever.

VICTORIA WAS grateful for the couch under her stomach because if she had been standing, she would've collapsed.

Jose had been right—his dragon was more animal than human. But as he pounded away, something inside her broke free, as if she'd been waiting for exactly this type of man her whole life.

Old Victoria never would've dug her nails into a man's wrist—probably drawing blood—and demand for him to take her harder.

And yet she'd done it without thinking.

Go back to a hesitant male who fumbled and never made her come?

Never.

Jose's voice—not as deep as just a minute before, making her wonder if his dragon had receded—asked, "Ready for more?" Strong hands lifted her up against his body, and he nuzzled her cheek. "Tell me what you want, and you'll have it, Tori."

"Is it Jose-Jose in charge now?"

He chuckled. "Yes, it's the human half. You were so wild and wicked for my dragon, that he decided to share."

Wild and wicked were never words used to describe Victoria before.

Yet, as she leaned back against the tall, strong man at her back, she wanted to be both those things. "So now it means I can compare the two of you?"

He twirled her around and clutched her against his front, taking her chin between thumb and forefinger. "Don't make this into a contest unless you're ready for the consequences."

She raised her brows, caution long thrown to the wind. "Maybe I am?"

With a growl, he took her lips, nibbling, licking, and eventually moving between them to lap and devour her mouth. Victoria gripped his shoulders, unafraid to dig in her nails, and kissed him back, moving her tongue against his, and even pressing her lower body against his already hardening cock.

He growled again into her mouth, the vibrations shooting down her body, ending between her thighs. Even though she'd just had him, not to mention two orgasms, she ached. Ached to have him inside her, feeling her, claiming her in the way only he could.

One of his hands moved down her side slowly, to her thigh, before lifting her leg and hitching it at his hip. He held it there as he moved his hips forward, the base of his shaft hitting her clit, making her cry out.

He broke the kiss and murmured, "Time for the other half of me to claim you, Tori. And when I'm done, you're going to have trouble standing."

Before she could taunt him, he lifted her ass and brought her up his body, until her legs wrapped around his waist. He distracted her with more kisses, devouring her mouth as if she was the most delicious, delectable taste in the world.

Between his tongue and his teeth, she barely registered her back coming against the wall. But as he pulled away a fraction only to return to slam close inside her, his cock filling her, she moaned.

He nipped her jaw. "That's right, my human, feel me inside you." He moved back and slammed in again. "You're about to learn just how a dragonman claims his female, his mate, his future."

Digging her heels into his back, she whispered, "Then stop talking."

His eyes flashed, but he took her lips again, swiping, licking, nibbling as he continued to thrust into her heat. She didn't even care about the wall at her back, loving how he kept her hips in place as he moved, to reposition her slightly with each movement, to reach deeper inside her.

Damn, she might truly walk funny after this. But Victoria didn't care. He was claiming her, branding her, letting her know that he wanted her.

And she loved it.

Not wanting to be only on the receiving end, she scraped her nails down his back. He growled, "More. Mark me. I want to feel it in the morning."

His naughty words snapped something inside her. She dug harder into his skin, this time also taking his bottom lip between her teeth and biting. Hard.

He retaliated by moving a hand between them and flicking her clit.

Victoria sucked in a breath, so sensitive from his movement and her previous orgasms that she nearly came right then and there.

Jose did it again, and she decided to make him feel

some delicious torture, too, by tightening her inner muscles.

He groaned. "You drive me so fucking crazy, Tori. Don't stop."

She didn't, loving how much closer she felt to him like this, holding him as he continued to stroke deep inside her.

His fingers started pinching, swiping and rubbing her clit. Within seconds she moaned, "I'm going to come."

"Then come, love. I'm here to hold you up as you do."

She let go, embracing the blinding pleasure, barely noting how Jose swallowed her cries with his mouth.

Between the attention of his tongue and his dick, she lingered in that plane of pleasure so close to pain for longer than she thought was possible.

And then he stilled, shouting into her mouth, and she could feel him coming, another orgasm washing over her.

Her entire body spasmed, the pleasure nearly too much for her to bear, making her cry out.

Just when she thought she'd break, bliss flooded her body and she slowly came down from the brink.

Jose placed gentle kisses on her lips, taking his time to savor her, as if it were the first and only time he'd have her.

When he finally pulled away, he moved to her ear and asked, "Ready to go again? My dragon wants another turn."

Even though she'd be beyond sore, and she was

already overwhelmed with all the orgasms, she knew this was important to him, to both man and dragon.

And besides, Victoria was afraid that if she said no, she might wake up from her delicious dream and be faced with reality again.

So she held onto him tighter and murmured, "Can he top that?"

Jose's voice dropped a fraction, to the tone she'd come to recognize as his inner beast. "This time, I won't hold back. You're mine, human. Mine."

And he somehow proved to be correct, the first of many, many attempts throughout the night and days to come, both sides of her dragonman forever trying to outdo the other.

Chapter Six

J ose woke up nearly two weeks later with the faint sunshine shining through the window and was careful to hold his female close but not too hard. Not only did she need her rest, but he also didn't want to wake his dragon, who would then want more sex to try and impregnate her.

Not that Jose didn't enjoy every inch of his mate, but he looked forward to when he could talk with her for hours, or even when he could introduce her to his family.

Because, yes, he wanted his family to like her.

Putting his nose where her shoulder met her neck, he took a deep inhale. The familiar scent of vanilla and female filled his senses, but there was a different undercurrent today. When he realized what it was—it smelled faintly of him—he froze.

His dragon stirred sleepily inside his mind. *Yes. She finally carries our young.*

Jose took a second to process it all.

Of course he knew the frenzy would only end when Victoria became pregnant, but it had been a dream—an end goal that was never quite in sight.

However, when his dragon dropped his head and went back to sleep inside his mind, it truly told him that it was done.

Jose would be a father in about nine months' time.

He pulled his female a little closer, closed his eyes, and smiled.

When he'd begrudgingly agreed to participate in the lottery, he'd known in the end he'd have a child and then be forced to raise it either alone or having his parents' help. He hadn't expected the human female to want him, let alone tempt him.

But now, with the female of his dreams asleep against him, he imagined being with her, raising their child, and building the future he'd never really thought he'd ever have.

And fuck, he wanted all of it. Even the late-night feedings, the diaper changes, the barely having enough energy to shower before falling asleep. Because he'd do it all with Victoria at his side. Not only because raising a child with his human was the dream he'd never knew he wanted, but the child would be pieces of her and him together, not to mention a visual reminder of how they were true mates.

His inner beast mumbled, *Maybe. But you still have to convince her to stay on PineRock.*

Jose frowned. That was another thing he hadn't really considered before, when it'd been some faceless female he'd have to fuck.

And suddenly, his confidence faltered a second. How the hell would he convince her to leave everything she knew, abandon her family and friends, and come live with the dragon-shifters on PineRock? He mostly loved his clan, but it was remote. And humans weren't allowed to visit whenever they felt like it, either.

But it wasn't like he could live with her in the human world. All dragon-shifters were required to live on a clan somewhere in the US—the government needing to keep track of them. While he didn't always like that, it wasn't as if he would do something stupid, like try to pass as a human to live with Tori in her home.

Her home. How much did he really know about it? All he could recall was that she lived in North Las Vegas from her contract, but nothing else about it. Sure, even the dragon-shifters knew about the casinos in Las Vegas proper, but he couldn't imagine his book-carrying female spending most of her time there.

While sex with his female was amazing, he needed more of her, to find out what she liked and didn't like.

Damn, he had some wooing to do, sort of like speed dating on crack, to get where he needed to be.

Victoria arched against him, and he felt the instant she woke up when she melted even further into his side. Despite the fact he'd lost count of how many times he'd had his mate over the last two weeks, her early morning voice stirred his cock from semihard to granite within seconds as she said, "Good morning. Is it Jose-Jose, or Mr. Dragon right now?"

He kissed her cheek. "Jose. My dragon is sleeping."

She glanced over at him. "Sleeping? Since when does he do that? Your beast barely allows *me* to sleep."

He turned her until Victoria was on her back. Caressing her cheek, he decided to be blunt and see how she reacted. Maybe not the most romantic way to go about it, but it would help him figure out how to move forward. "He's asleep because the frenzy's over." He moved his hand over her lower abdomen. "You're carrying our baby."

She blinked the last of sleep from her eyes before they widened. "So I'm pregnant?"

A smile tugged his lips. "Either that or very, very good at hiding your own scent from a dragon-shifter. Which, I might add, would be something new."

She lightly hit his chest, and the playful gesture relaxed him a fraction. If she could be playful, she wasn't freaking out.

Victoria replied, "Aren't you supposed to be super nice to me now?"

He moved his hand up her body, lazily kneaded her breast, and finally ended by cupping her cheek. "Nice would be boring to a female who likes to mark with her nails."

She raised her brows. "Hey, I won't apologize for that. You asked for it."

65

He nipped her bottom lip. "I did, and don't ever stop doing it."

He waited to see if his hint of the future would make her nervous, hesitate, or some other negative sign.

However, she merely rolled into him and hitched her leg over his hip. "Then, Baby Daddy, I want to go back to sleep."

Jose could leave it at that, but that would be the coward's way out. So he tilted her head until she met his gaze. "Are you okay with it all? And yes, I know it was the whole point of the lottery, but there's a difference between words on a page and the real thing."

She smiled slowly. "You taught me that, didn't you?"

She was referring to the summary warning about dragon-shifters. Apparently, they needed to add "wild, growly, and delicious" to the description.

"I mean it, Tori. I'll have to call ADDA later today, and then reality sets in beyond this cabin."

Placing a hand on his chest, she lightly stroked her fingers, unaware of how each pass made him want to toss her back and take her all over again.

Seriously, he would *never* get enough of his female.

She finally spoke again. "As long as you don't ditch me as soon as we get to Clan PineRock, then I think I can face reality just fine."

"Don't even suggest I'd abandon you," he growled.

Though he wanted to say more—that he wanted her as his mate forever, and that it wouldn't take much more for him to fall in love with her.

But even Jose knew not to push too much too soon. That was another thing that had caused the other dragonman's mate to run and leave him in misery.

As if sensing his dragon stirring at her comment, she traced his jaw before leaning up to kiss him briefly. "Of course you won't." She smiled at him, the sight making his heart skip a beat. She added, "Although maybe we could take a shower together before you call ADDA? As much as I enjoyed the frenzy, it'd be nice to explore you slowly. With my tongue."

His cock let out a drop of moisture at her statement. He'd been the one to win the lottery, not Victoria.

He kissed her slowly, taking his time to explore her mouth and loving how she melted with each stroke. He finally pulled away. "As my female wishes."

With that, he pulled her out of bed and guided her toward the bathroom.

THE END of the frenzy hadn't fully sunk in yet, but Victoria wanted to steal whatever time she had left with her dragonman in this cabin, away from everything else.

The aftermath would come crashing down soon enough—especially the part about her being pregnant and her having to live with a dragon clan for at least nine months.

But right here, right now, she wanted to spend a little

time with her man without the frenzy demanding sex and more sex.

So she allowed Jose to lead her into the bathroom. She watched his broad shoulders and back as he turned on the shower, adjusting the temperature, and finally turning back toward her with heat in his eyes.

Even after all the hours and hours of sex they'd had, he still wanted her.

And that made her belly flip, in a good way.

She only hoped the feeling stuck around, especially once they got to know each other better. Would the sexy dragonman find her boring outside the bedroom?

No. She wouldn't allow doubts to invade the moment. Right now, it was just her and Jose, naked and ready to explore one another without some instinctual need driving their actions.

Jose closed the distance between them and ran a hand down her side, his slightly rough hand making her shiver. He murmured, "Do you want to explore first or should I?"

The deep huskiness of his voice boosted her confidence and she pushed back her shoulders, loving how his gaze darted to her breasts. She replied, "I'll go first. After all, you've tasted me and I have yet to do the same to you."

A mate-claim frenzy had been about sex, and more sex, but none of the oral variety. Apparently, Jose's inner dragon had really wanted only one thing—to get her pregnant. And sadly, a tongue and fingers wouldn't do the job.

Not that she would hold it against the beast. She rather liked his instinctual side at times.

Taking her hand, Jose moved to the shower. "Then hurry up. The sooner you're done, the sooner I can have my turn. One taste of your sweet honey wasn't nearly enough."

The promise in his words made wetness rush between her thighs. Yep, she still believed he had some sort of special dragon-shifter pheromone or magical ability to make her want him so damn much.

Once the hot water hit her body, Victoria let out a moan. She was only human, and therefore very, very sore. Turning this way and then that way, she took a few minutes to soothe every ache.

Jose growled. "You should be taking a bath and relaxing after the frenzy. You don't have to do this."

She turned toward him, touched by his concern. He'd tried his best to let her sleep when needed during the frenzy, but it seemed as if his caring would last beyond it, too. Which made her forget a little more about her aching body. "It's not a matter of *having* to do anything but *wanting* to do it." Running a hand down his chest, she murmured boldly—something she never would've done a few weeks ago, "I've been dreaming of taking your cock between my lips for days."

Jose grabbed his erection and stroked once. "You're

too good to be true, love. I keep thinking I'll wake up from the best dream of my life."

There he went, saying sweet things again. Deep down, her growly dragonman was turning out to be so much more.

Victoria let her hand stray further down his abdomen until she met his fingers on his cock. "Now, let go and let me take control of this."

Her strong dragonman obeyed, and she smiled. Yes, she liked Jose dominating her for the most part in bed, but there was something about occasionally being in control, too, that simply felt right with her.

As her hand stroked up and then teased the tip of his shaft with her forefinger, Jose placed a hand on the tile wall and leaned against it for support. "I'm not going to last long if you keep that up, Tori."

"The dragonman who lasted at least two hours at one point is about to come this easily?" She tsked. "Maybe you're getting old."

His pupils flashed. "I'm tempted to show you how well this old man can handle you."

Since Jose was only in his early thirties, she resisted laughing.

However, she wasn't going to be distracted from what she'd wanted from the first day when Jose had gone down on her.

So Victoria kissed his chest, one of his nipples, and continued downward until she reached the trail of hair that led to her final destination.

She crouched down until she was on her knees, putting his cock right in front of her face. She leaned over and licked the slit on the tip, loving the tang of saltiness there.

Jose bucked his hips, nearly shoving his shaft into her face.

With one lick, she had so much power over him.

And it felt wonderful.

Gripping the base of his cock, she leaned over and placed light kisses on the tip and then down the side. When she finally rubbed her cheek against the soft-yet-steely length, Jose placed a hand in her hair. "Please, love, suck me deep. I'm dying to know what your mouth feels like."

Maybe someone else would make him beg, but Victoria was too eager. She'd never wanted to taste a man so much in her life, almost as if she didn't suck him deep, she'd feel empty until she did.

She finally took him into her mouth, loving how hot he was under her tongue. As if she'd done this a thousand times before, she moved her hand on the bottom half of his dick as she bobbed her head up and down, careful to lave with her tongue as she went.

Using her other hand, she fondled his balls, which made Jose press her head more against his dick.

No shy man afraid to tell her what he wanted.

Maybe he'd be that way in every facet of life.

As he dug his nails lightly into her scalp, Victoria forgot about everything but moving her head, teasing his shaft, and finally, she stopped fondling his balls to stroke herself. Merely rubbing once made her moan around Jose's cock.

Her dragonman's gravelly voice filled the shower. "Fuck, yes, make yourself come at the same time, my demanding human. Keep saying—" He groaned. "—and taking what you want."

Maybe if she wasn't on the verge of coming, she'd think about how that wasn't true most of the time. Only with him.

However, as Jose moved his hips and Victoria felt herself about to break, he stilled and growled, his seed spurting into her mouth. She didn't hesitate to swallow as he did, loving the saltiness that was Jose.

The taste was what sent her into her own orgasm. She cried out around his shaft and barely noticed how Jose moved back and slowly brought her to her feet.

He held her close, and she finally slumped against him, the hot water cascading over them both.

Pressing his cheek against her head, he murmured, "You please me too well, my little mate."

Pride surged through her. Never had she thought giving a guy a blow job would make her feel so good.

Then a question hit her, one she couldn't hold back. "Will the frenzy come back again, once the baby is born, in a never-ending cycle?"

Because if so, she wasn't sure if she could handle it over and over again for the rest of her life.

He stroked her back. "No, love. Just the once." He

moved to her ear. "Although if you think I'm not going to remember you digging your nails into my back, my ass, my arms, and ask you to do it every time, then you're crazy."

She smiled against the warm skin of his chest. "Good, because I don't know if I can go back to not marking my man."

He growled. "I like you calling me your male."

Victoria hadn't realized she'd done it. But it felt right, no matter how strange and short their courtship.

Before she could reply, he finally lifted her head to meet his gaze, her heart skipping a beat at the approval she saw there. "We have a lot to talk about, but let's clean up and get things taken care of with ADDA first." He traced her bottom lip. "But in case you start to worry, or freak out about your situation, then promise me that you'll tell me. I don't want you to hold anything back from me. Ever."

The longer she was around Jose, the more she wondered how every human woman out there didn't go racing for their own dragon-shifter. She'd never seen a man so devoted so quickly.

She nodded. "Okay, I promise. Once we're alone again after the ADDA stuff and are settled on your clan's land, I have a ton of questions to ask. I had them even before all of this, and now? I may never get to ask them all."

He traced her cheek. "Even if it takes my whole life, I'll answer them all, Tori. You'll see."

The confidence in his voice, as if he believed it, made her heart skip a beat. She wanted to believe they would have a happily ever after of their own, and yet, it was never easy for a human and dragon-shifter to stay together in the US. At least, what she'd read to date, anyway.

Maybe they would be the exception instead of the rule.

Of course, to make that a reality, she needed to make an effort, too. It couldn't all fall to Jose. So she blurted, "How about you just start by telling me how to win your family over? Or, at the very least, how to make a good first impression?"

He searched her gaze, approval burning strong. "You want to win over my family?"

"Of course," she stated. "I want my—no, *our*—child to know all of their family. Mine might be more difficult since my parents live all the way in Scottsdale in Arizona, but I'm sure we can find a way for them to visit, too. It will probably be the strangest Christmas or Thanksgiving in history, but even so, I'm going to make it work."

Especially since half dragon-shifters could rarely go off a clan's land without permission, and her child would be one.

For a split second, she wondered how the dragons dealt with so little freedom.

But then she pushed it aside. That was a conversation to have with Jose later. Getting to his clan, learning the ropes, and getting used to the idea of living with a dragon clan were her main goals right now.

Oh, not to mention the teensy little fact she was *pregnant*—inner dragons could almost never lie about that fact—and would be a mom before long.

Placing a hand over her lower abdomen, she tried to believe it was real and imagine a tiny person growing inside her. However, at this stage, it was merely Jose's word telling her so.

He placed his much larger hand over hers, his warmth an instant comfort. She met his gaze as he said, "I'll be with you the whole way, love. It'll be all right in the end."

It was the closest either of them had hinted about the reality of a human birthing a half-dragon-shifter baby— in other words, there was a chance, about a fifty-fifty chance, she could die.

Jose kissed her cheek and said, "Your chances are much better than they would've been a few years ago. As much as I hate to admit it, those bloody British dragon-shifters have been busy figuring out how to keep their human mates alive, even with having more children than dragons usually have in such a short time period. If I have to make a deal with PineRock's head doctor to make sure he finds out why—if he doesn't know already —I'll do it. I want my true mate for more than nine months."

Since Victoria didn't know much beyond the book and the new videocast that had slowly started to introduce dragon-shifter culture to humans, she had no idea what he was talking about. She echoed, "My chances are better now?"

"Yes, love. Much better. The Brits haven't lost any human mates in childbirth for nearly two years." He kissed her lips slowly before adding, "I'll tell you everything once I get the chance to better know my mate. But in order to do that, we need to get to PineRock." He picked up a shampoo bottle. "Now, let me help you get clean and we'll do exactly that."

Victoria had never thought a man helping to wash her hair would be so rewarding, but as he massaged her scalp and she leaned her forehead against his chest, she thought it was something she could get used to.

And she was so relaxed from Jose's ministrations that she barely thought about anything but the dragonman in front of her and how she already wanted to stay with him beyond the birth of their child.

Chapter Seven

V ictoria tried her best to focus on the scenery during the car ride to Clan PineRock instead of staring at the dragonman beside her.

It was difficult, and she did steal a few glances, but as long as he held her hand, Victoria could at least attempt to memorize her new landscape. Growing up in and around Las Vegas, she was used to the desert—sand, brush, and yes, even cacti. Not to mention lots and lots of rocks.

However, while Lake Tahoe itself was famous for being a deep lake in a beautiful shade of blue, she'd never really thought much about the surrounding area. The tall, thin pine trees, the ridges with little greenery at the top but occasionally snow—even in late summer—and the chance waterfall here and there were beautiful.

And as they drove deeper into the Desolation Wilderness, an area to the west of Lake Tahoe, Victoria fell in love with the forests and mountains. So very different from back home.

She wondered for the first time if dragon-shifters ever carried humans in the air. She could only imagine how much more beautiful an aerial view would be in winter when snow covered everything and some of the smaller lakes nearby would freeze, although never Tahoe itself.

Jose squeezed her hand and she met his gaze. He motioned up ahead. "There's the entrance to PineRock."

Leaning forward, she tried her best to see it from the back seat.

There was a huge metal gate in front of what looked like an entrance carved into rock. "I never saw anything about you living inside the mountain."

"No, we don't. Just wait. I don't want to ruin the surprise."

She was about to demand more when the gate opened slowly and the ADDA employee Ashley drove them through it, into the carved-out tunnel.

About forty feet later, they emerged into a huge valley —or maybe some sort of clearing? Victoria didn't know the right term—surrounded by mountains on all sides. Within the open space lay various houses and buildings. She could just make out a black dragon launching from the ground into the sky.

Jose murmured, "Welcome to PineRock."

As another dragon soared down and then landed—a golden one—she wanted to burst from the car and run to see him or her shift into a human.

Yes, they'd be naked at the end of it, but she didn't care. She'd never seen anyone shift before, nor even had the chance to ask about it.

Did it hurt? How often could they do it? Could they ever get stuck in one form or the other?

But now, it was possible. Or, at the very least, soon would be.

Of course, that reminded her of the dragonman next to her. Somehow tearing her gaze away from the mismatched cabins, houses, and taller buildings of indiscriminate nature, she asked, "Will you show me your dragon form soon?"

Jose grunted an affirmative. "Yes, once we get settled. Believe me, my inner beast is anxious to come out and even threatening to shift right now."

The ADDA employee spoke up from the driver's seat. "I'd rather not have my car turn into a crushed pile of metal, thank you very much." Ashley pulled in front of one of the larger buildings that had four or five stories. It could've been a store or a sort of central government building, if Victoria had to guess. Did dragon-shifters have such things? The book had been about British dragon clans, not American ones. And there were bound to be differences.

Ashley turned off the engine and added, "We're here. Now before you two run off to get into trouble, we have a few things to settle first. And I'm sure your clan leader wouldn't appreciate you ditching him before introducing his latest resident, Jose."

Victoria didn't know much about the clan leader, apart from the fact his name was Wes Dalton. "We won't run off. Yet."

Jose snorted. "Wes isn't as fussy as ADDA. As long as you're with me, Tori, he probably won't care."

Ashley sniffed. "Probably being the operative word. Regardless, I don't want him chewing out my ass to my boss." She opened her door. "Now are you going to stick with me or do I have to call a few of the Protectors to make sure you do?"

Protectors were a type of security guard for dragon-shifters, that much she knew from the official ADDA website. Although they often trained with the US Army Reserves and were much more than an average rent-a-cop. Victoria knew she'd never want to meet a dragon warrior in the sky, or even on the ground. Their super senses alone would win them most any fight.

Victoria answered before Jose. "We'll stick with you, Ashley. I'm curious to meet the clan leader anyway."

Especially since he will ultimately be the one to decide if I stay here after the baby is born or not.

They disembarked the car. Jose took her hand again and they followed Ashley into the building.

Victoria did her best not to gape, but failed. A lot of men and even a few women walked around in T-shirts, their dark, inked dragon tattoos on their arms identical. Every single one of them had to be at least six feet tall, even the women. And they all had more muscle than she'd ever seen in one room before, even when she'd attempted to join a gym for a few weeks.

She felt somewhat powerless among them all, too. They all had super senses to augment their strength.

Victoria just needed to make sure she never pissed anyone off she couldn't handle in the end.

A few of the dragon-shifters nodded at Jose, and he grunted back. There were so many faces, she wondered how long it'd take her to learn them all. Because even if they tried to ignore her, Victoria would learn their names. Before she'd become an online teacher, she'd been one with a real-life classroom. And learning everyone's names as soon as possible had been a huge help, her making the effort at least scoring a few points with the students.

Ashley stopped in front of a door. "And here we are. Wes and a few other prominent clan members will be inside. Ready, Victoria? Or do you need a minute?"

Doing her best to ignore her pounding heart—she wanted to meet the clan leader but was still a little nervous since her experience with dragon-shifters was limited to one—she nodded. "I'm ready."

"Then let's get this over with," the other human woman stated.

Ashley entered the room and walked in as if she owned it, her head and shoulders high, her gait determined. Victoria had to give the woman credit—she didn't let much stronger, taller, and faster beings intimidate her. Maybe she could learn something from the ADDA employee.

Once inside, Victoria spotted a slightly older, mildly tanned auburn-haired man with the universal American dragon-shifter tattoo on his arm, leaning back in his chair. To his right was another man, with dark hair, skin, and the same tattoo, as well as a dark-haired female with light brown skin to the center man's left. However, since the woman wore a long-sleeved shirt, Victoria had no idea if she was a dragon-shifter or not.

Then her pupils flashed to slits. Yep, a dragon-shifter.

Ashley nodded to the auburn-haired man. "Dalton."

So he was Wes Dalton, the clan leader.

He motioned for them all to sit. "A pleasure, as always, Ms. Swift." His brown-eyed gaze moved to Victoria. "And you must be Victoria."

Even as they sat, Jose placed a possessive arm around her shoulders. She wanted to frown at him, but she didn't want to be rude to the clan leader. "Yes, that's me. Nice to meet you, Mr. Dalton."

The woman across from her snorted. "So polite."

Wes frowned at the dragonwoman. "Behave, Cris. Her safety is your concern now." Before Victoria could ask what he meant, Wes waved at the woman. "This is Cristina Juarez, our head Protector. She's in charge of clan security."

Victoria blinked. "A female head Protector?"

The woman leaned forward. "Is that a problem?"

Jose growled. "Be nice, Cris."

Cris raised her brows. "I can be nice later. Her safety is more important, which means understanding my role here. I can't have her doubting my authority or ignoring my orders, because that might get her killed."

The man to Wes's right sighed. "Ignore Cris. It's not easy being a female Protector, let alone a head one. She comes off as aggressive, but she cares deeply for the clan." Cris growled at him in warning, but the man ignored her. "My name is Troy Carter, and I'm the clan's head doctor. You'll be seeing me more than probably anyone else on PineRock, apart from Jose, of course."

She nodded at the doctor, grateful for his smile and kind eyes. Not everyone would hate her here, it seemed.

The clan leader spoke again. "And just call me Wes, Victoria. Mr. Dalton sounds like my father." He leaned forward and continued, "With the introductions out of the way, let's get down to business. Victoria, you're to stay here until the baby is born. After that, you'll have an option of staying, but only if you convince us three that you truly want to be here, regardless of the consequences. Not even for Jose's dragon's sake will I force someone to live with us." Jose tightened his grip on Victoria's shoulders, but the clan leader carried on unfazed. "Which means you'll have to abide by the clan rules above all. There's no halfway point here—you're either with the clan or outside of it. Do you understand?"

Even though Wes's eyes were kind, they were also steely. She could only imagine what happened if someone dared to piss him off.

Which, of course, she had zero interest in doing. She wouldn't stand a chance against an angry dragon-shifter, and that was before they changed into a big, scaled beast.

She nodded. Wes then waved to either side of him. "Cris and Dr. Carter will help coordinate your stay at the beginning. But after that, you'll have lessons with the clan teachers, as well as learn plenty of stuff from Jose and his family. However, if for any reason you feel threatened or in danger, you come straight to me, okay?"

Jose growled. "I will protect her."

Wes moved his gaze to him. "I know that's your intent. But it's just a precaution and the standard protocol. You know that. Even if Victoria is the first human to live on PineRock for quite some time and is your true mate, the rules haven't changed."

She frowned at that, and something hit her. "Are there any other humans here?"

Wes shook his head. "You're the only one."

"Oh." She'd assumed at least some of the dragons had human mates.

Which meant she'd be completely surrounded by a different species, with their own ways and expectations. No one else would truly understand her situation, let alone would she have a friend with whom she could rant a little when she got frustrated.

Sure, she wanted to make this work with Jose, but there were always times when a girl needed to vent a little. And she doubted they'd let her reach out to her human best friend back in Vegas.

Could she handle the isolation?

As if sensing her slightly rising panic, Ashley said, "After a few months, you can have visitors, provided they pass the background check. Not to mention I'll be stopping by often to check on you, so much so that everyone will get sick of me soon enough."

Even though she hadn't known the ADDA employee long, Victoria already liked her. "I doubt that'll happen."

Jose grunted. "Oh, it will."

Ashley gave him a glance before looking back at the clan leader. "I have all the paperwork with me. Shall we go get this the hell over with?"

Wes's lips twitched. "I should report your unprofessional attitude to ADDA."

"But won't. You never did before."

As they shared a look, Victoria wondered at their history.

However, Ashley stood up and everyone else followed suit. Wes looked back at Victoria. "Jose will show you to your cabin, but know that you have appointments with both Cris and Dr. Carter later today. The sooner you know what to expect, the sooner you can try to establish a routine. From what I understand, you'll be working while living here."

She bobbed her head. "I teach online high school classes. They'll be starting up soon, and I want to keep it up."

"As long as you don't divulge secrets, that'll be fine. But the second you cause trouble, you'll have to quit."

His edict rubbed her the wrong way, but she had no choice but to accept it. Her future, the one where she could stay with her child, dangled in the balance. "I understand."

"Good. Then I'm off to fill out paperwork with Ms. Swift. Welcome to Clan PineRock, Victoria Lewis. I hope you'll think of it as home soon enough."

Once Wes and Ashley were gone, Jose hugged her against his side. He said to the other dragon-shifters, "Text me the appointments and I'll make sure Tori gets there on time."

Before either could say a word, he whisked her out of the room and back toward the entrance. He whispered into her ear, "I'll show you to our new place before you meet anyone else."

"Our place?" she echoed. "I thought it was my own place."

"It is, but if you think I'm going to live apart from you after the last two weeks, then I didn't try hard enough to convince you how much I want you."

Her cheeks heated a fraction. She wanted Jose nearby, but she couldn't resist teasing him. "Maybe you *do* need to try harder."

His pupils flashed. "If you didn't need a small break to recover, I'd show you at the first opportunity. But just know that I'm going to be planning a mind-blowing night for tomorrow. Maybe then you'll finally understand how much I want you."

Her heart rate kicked up at the same time heat surged

through her body. Despite the fact she was sore, tired, and hungry from the frenzy, she still wanted more of her dragonman.

She probably always would.

Not now, Tori. She needed to focus on fitting in with the clan, too. "Until then, show me as much of the clan as possible." She paused and added, "And your dragon, too."

"A demanding female." His voice dropped a fraction. "I like it."

Holy crap, this man was almost too perfect for words.

Maybe she needed to meet his family after all, to make him more real and reveal some flaws. After all, families often had embarrassing stories, ones she couldn't wait to hear.

But as he steered her toward her new home, she studied every little thing about her surroundings, from the houses to the paths and streetlamp. For some reason, most Americans had a medieval vision of dragon-shifter living, but they were as modern as a human's.

To ensure she didn't forget anything, Victoria would need to start taking notes. She had no aspirations about writing a book, but if any other human came to Pine-Rock, it could help.

Chapter Eight

It took every bit of restraint Jose possessed not to find some dark, hidden corner and take his female again.

Even without the frenzy, he wanted her constantly.

His inner dragon spoke up. *Let her rest a little. And remember, she was curious about dragon-shifters from the moment we met her. Indulge that, and she'll adore us more.*

It seemed his dragon wanted to please their human, too.

They stepped outside the building into the afternoon sunshine. He'd just turned them toward the cabin meant to be hers when he heard a familiar female voice behind him. "Woo-hoo, Jose."

His sister.

Turning around, sure enough, there stood Gaby, her highlighted hair loose around her shoulders and wearing a grin as she darted her dark brown eyes between him and Victoria. He growled, "What do you want, Gaby?"

"To meet your human." She studied them a second. "It seems you owe me a huge debt for making you go through with the lottery."

"What is she talking about?" Victoria asked.

He decided the truth was best. "This is my younger sister, Gabriella, although everyone calls her Gaby. She's the one who entered us into the lottery, without my permission, I might add."

"Your sister?" The faint surprise in her voice was expected as he and his sister didn't look much alike. Victoria walked forward and put out a hand. "I'm glad to meet you. Call me Tori."

With a bemused look, Gaby took her hand and shook. "Not as much as I am. And judging by my brother's growly, protective demeanor, I assume you're going to stay on PineRock with us long-term?"

He narrowed his eyes. "Don't put her on the spot, Gabriella."

His sister ignored him. "Are you? If so, then we should definitely get acquainted in the next week or so, to plot and conspire against my brother. I leave for my own lottery stint in less than two weeks, but I'm sure there's a lot we can do before then."

Victoria replied, "Oh, that's right. All dragon siblings participate in the lottery."

Gaby bobbed her head. "Yep, that's why I owed my brother a huge favor for going through with it. But I'm guessing it's repaid now that he has you."

Victoria's cheek heated. She murmured, "You can tell I'm his true mate?"

"I wish I was that good. But, alas, no. The clan leader let me and my parents know that Jose found his true mate. That way, we could prepare you a better welcome and all."

Jose walked over to Victoria and pulled her against his side. "I was going to bring her by the house a little later. At least let me show Tori her new home before you start your interrogations."

Gaby put up her hands. "Okay. Geez, you don't have to bite off my head, brother." Gaby looked back at Victoria. "I'll see you later today, probably at dinner. My mom is working on quite the feast. And if I were you, I'd make sure to wear some looser clothing because she'll keep feeding you until you're about to puke."

Jose turned him and Victoria a fraction more away from Gaby. "Then we need to go and make sure her luggage arrived to heed your advice, Gaby."

With that, Jose guided his mate away. Behind them, Gaby shouted, "I love you too, brother!"

He sighed, and Victoria snorted. "I like your sister."

"And that's what scares me," he muttered.

"So we're going to dinner at your parents' house tonight then?"

"I know it's really soon and while I can put them off if need be, they'll just find a way to accidentally drop by. A dinner, to meet them all at once, might be the best route."

Victoria shook her head. "No, it's okay. I'd rather get it out of the way if I'm honest. The sooner I know how people view a human living here, the better I can make plans on how to adapt."

His female was truly remarkable, ready to fight her own battles to be accepted. "You don't have to make all of the adjustments. If Wes's plans go the way he wants, there will be more humans living here in the coming years. And the more accepting PineRock is with you, the easier it'll be to entice others."

"Entice, huh? Given that two hundred women showed up to that hotel ballroom merely for the chance to have at you, I think it wouldn't be that hard."

Jose shook his head. "There's a difference between those who want to brag they've fucked a dragon-shifter and those who truly want to get to know us and stay."

Victoria tilted her head. "I'll admit I don't know as much as I should about humans living with dragon clans, but there are a number of other clans nearby, right? Are there humans there? I only ask because I'd like the chance to talk to them and maybe learn."

He sighed. "We haven't been as close as we could have been with the other three dragon clans in the greater Tahoe area. But if anyone would know about humans living with dragon mates on StoneRiver, SkyTree, or StrongFalls, it would be Cris. The Protectors, at least, talk with one another out of necessity to keep this territory safe. You can ask her when you see her in an hour or so."

"Maybe."

He didn't like the uncertainty in Victoria's tone. "Look, Cris can appear over the top at first, but she loves the clan with all she has. As long as you don't question her being head Protector—she gets a shit time of it because she's female—then she might warm up to you."

"So if female head Protectors are rare, are there ever any female clan leaders?"

His mate was a curious thing, and he hoped to indulge her often. "There's at least one I know of, in Ireland. And a recent pair—one female and one male—took control of a clan in England and are leading it together. But I only know of those two instances because of reports in the media and online. Many clans are still secretive, especially to outsiders. Hell, there's not even a meeting place—online or in real life—for clan leaders to share information."

Only in recent years had Jose even really thought about it all. For as long as he could remember, clans kept to themselves. Then that human female in England had published her book about dragon-shifters, and things had begun to change.

His dragon spoke up. *But you can't be mad about it. That book brought us our Tori.*

True. I do wish I had more answers for our mate, though. While I'm sure she can win over Gaby, it's going to take time for the others to accept her. And while I want to think we are enough for her, she may get lonely without female friends.

Don't make such gloomy predictions. Our mate is smart and determined. I'm sure she'll figure it out.

I hope so, dragon. I hope so.

The small cabin meant for Victoria came into view, and he focused on his mate and how she'd react, nothing else. He gestured ahead. "That's to be yours—although I still say ours."

She grinned as she took it in. "It's so cute, and truly a cabin, not like the other ginormous place."

He eyed the single-story log cabin with a fireplace and a covered front porch.

While it may be too small if they had more than one child, it would be cozy and perfect for him, Victoria, and their baby on the way. "There's a backyard, too. And it's not far from the small lake we have for the clan's use."

She raised an eyebrow. "Please don't tell me you dive into the lake in the wintertime."

He shrugged one shoulder. "Dragons don't feel the cold as much as humans do. And they like to be clean."

Anticipation burned in her gaze. "Maybe I can help wash him soon?"

Yes, please, his beast purred.

Victoria laughed. "Your pupils changed and then you frowned. He said yes, didn't he?"

He reached a hand up and caressed her cheek. "You're getting too good at reading me, love."

She leaned closer, her voice turning husky. "After nearly two weeks of a constant battle between your human and dragon halves, I'd like to think I've gotten to know both well."

His dragon shook out his wings. *She accepts both of us so easily. She belongs with us.*

I couldn't agree more, dragon.

They reached the porch, and Jose opened the door. Since they were on PineRock, he knew it was secure already and didn't hesitate to gesture inside. "Welcome to your new home, Tori. Hopefully before long, you'll call it *our* home."

She smiled at him a beat before dashing inside.

He couldn't help but chuckle at her enthusiasm before following.

As she turned around, her eyes wide as they took in the front room with its large fireplace, sofa, and a few other pieces of furniture, both man and beast stood a little taller. Their mate liked their new home.

"I love it, Jose. I've never had a house of my own before. Where's the backyard?"

He motioned and she dashed out back. As if he were on a leash, he followed her out, only to find her twirling in a circle with her arms outspread.

The sight made his heart skip a beat. He fucking loved everything about his female.

Her cheeks pink, she rushed up to him, took his hand, and tugged him toward the large lawn area. "Will your dragon fit here? Please say yes. I really want to see him before I do all the appointments. Not to mention it seems unfair not to see your dragon before I meet the rest of the family. Especially given how many times he claimed me."

His dragon stood tall and roared. *There's enough room. Let me out. I want to feel her scratch behind my ears.*

Okay, okay, just hold on. Let me explain things to her first since you can't talk in dragon form.

What I wouldn't give to be able to communicate telepathically.

That would probably drive his mate crazy over time, as his beast would probably broadcast sex fantasies nonstop.

But as he reveled in the pure anticipation and eagerness on Victoria's face, he decided maybe he *would* surprise her the first time.

He gestured toward the small back porch. "Stand over there until I finish shifting. Then you can come up to me, okay?"

She ran to the porch, put her hands on the railing, and leaned forward.

Never had he imagined a human leaning forward in anticipation, wanting to see his dragon would make him fall a little in love with her.

It's because she accepts all of us. Now, strip and let's get started.

In agreement, Jose moved to a good spot and quickly shucked off his clothes.

Victoria held her breath as Jose took off his clothes.

Partially it was because of his muscular, tan chest and powerful thighs. Not to mention the delicious dragon tattoo on one of his biceps and the large part of his anatomy she'd grown rather fond of between his legs.

A naked Jose Santos would steal her breath any day.

But it was more than that. For the first time ever, she was going to see not only a dragon-shifter change from human to dragon, but also meet Jose's dragon form.

Over the course of the frenzy, she'd come to accept both halves of him. But her curiosity always wondered what the dragon looked like. Merely knowing he was blue wasn't enough.

His dark brown eyes met hers and then he smiled. A few beats later, his body gave off a faint glow and he stretched out his limbs, his legs morphing into powerful hind legs complete with talons, his nose and jaw elongating into a snout, and large, beautiful wings grew from his back.

It probably didn't take more than thirty seconds or so, but it had almost played out in slow motion, to the point she still couldn't believe what she'd seen.

There now stood a nearly twenty-foot blue dragon, his scales slightly iridescent in the midmorning sunshine, in her backyard.

She almost pinched herself to make sure it was real. If she hadn't gone through the frenzy, she probably would have.

When he stretched out his wings, which were slightly transparent against the sunlight, and tilted his head down, his large, almond-shaped dragon eyes, complete with slitted pupils, looked straight at her.

It felt as if he were staring deep down into the hidden parts of her mind and heart.

And when he moved his head the other way and back, his scales reflecting even more sunshine, almost as if he were a precious gemstone, she nearly gasped. Beautiful, gorgeous, majestic—none of those words seemed enough to describe her man in his dragon form.

Jose motioned with a forelimb, and it snapped Victoria from her amazement. It was time to meet her man's dragon.

She half ran toward him, stopping just a few feet away. So she wouldn't have to strain her neck, the dragon lowered his head to nearly her eye level. Victoria extended a hand, debating whether to reach up or wait. But then the dragon closed the distance and butted his snout against her palm. When he moved his head, to guide her hand to his jaw, she smiled. "Are you a dragon or more like a cat or dog? Both like to have their jaws scratched."

The dragon blew a puff of air at her and she laughed. Victoria had known dragon-shifters couldn't speak in their dragon forms and had wondered how they communicated.

But it seemed Jose's beast had a way.

She absently ran her hand along the side of the dragon's snout, loving how the scales were mostly smooth with slight grooves to them, almost as if they were embossed leather. When she finally reached behind his ear, her fingers found a smooth patch of skin, without the scales. She scratched, and the dragon began to hum.

"Oh, so you are like a cat or dog then, wanting your ears scratched."

The dragon was too happy and leaned into the touch. Victoria added her other hand and scratched a little harder.

The dragon emitted what sounded like a groan, and she laughed. "I guess I know how to win you over."

Jose's dragon moved his head to lightly butt her shoulder. "What? You like it, right? So I'll just keep my ear scratches for special occasions."

With a low grunt, the dragon stood and picked her up around her middle with his front paw. Even though the dragon could easily crush her or skewer her with the large, sharp talons, Jose didn't hurt her. She instinctively knew he never would.

As he stared at her with one large, yellow eye, she said, "Maybe one day you could take me flying?" The dragon started to shake his head, but she added, "After the baby is born, of course."

Jose's beast almost smiled and nodded.

But then it all made her realize that one day her child would be able to change into a dragon, too. How was she supposed to raise a child that could change shape and fly away, with her not being able to follow?

And what else wouldn't she be able to teach them or help them with since she was only human?

As if sensing her mood, the dragon put her down, took a few steps back, and within seconds, had shrunk back into Jose's naked human form.

He engulfed her in a hug and asked, "What's wrong, love? Tell me."

Despite snuggling deeper against his chest, she said, "You didn't have to change back yet."

"I can morph into a dragon any time I want. It's not a once a day sort of thing." He moved his head back until he could look into her eyes. "Your expression turned wary and a little sad just now. And know this—a good dragon mate would never simply allow his female to remain sad and not try to make her happy again."

Her mood lightened a fraction. "And now whose reading me so well after such a short time?"

"Tori," he growled.

If there was to be anything between them—and Victoria hoped there would be—then she wouldn't hold back. "I was just thinking about our child shifting and flying away. How am I supposed to raise someone like that? It's not like I could catch them or play with them in the sky."

He cupped her cheek and stroked it slowly with his thumb. "It will take some strategic planning and help from others, but humans do it with half dragon-shifter children all over the world. Just like Melanie Hall-MacLeod."

The author of the book, the one she'd love nothing

better than to read a million times and then call up the woman to ask some questions.

Not that she would be able to do the latter. The woman was off trying to change laws and perceptions of dragons in her own country and beyond.

Maybe someday she'd find someone closer to her new home.

Jose pressed gently against her lower back, and she replied, "It's silly, I know. Don't worry about me. I'll be fine."

"No, it's not silly—it's going to be a huge challenge, I won't deny it. However, my family and I will be there. And if I have to barge into Wes's office and demand he contact every clan within an easy flying distance to find a human mated to a dragon-shifter, so you can have someone to talk to, then I'll do it."

As she stared at the determination in Jose's eyes, she knew he would, too. He really was unlike any man she'd known before.

And if he kept it up, she'd fall for him completely without even learning one embarrassing childhood story.

Chapter Nine

Victoria survived Cris's extensive lecture about clan rules—she even had a thick tome to read through—as well as Dr. Carter's exhaustive questions about her health. While she didn't know either one well enough to judge if they'd merely tolerate her or actually warm up to her, they at least treated her respectfully and not with disdain—she'd read online that some dragon-shifters didn't like humans *at all*—which she'd take for now.

Once done with both appointments, Jose insisted she take a quick nap, but now she walked next to her dragon-man, trying to dredge up the strength to be nice and charming for his family.

Since being charming didn't come naturally, Victoria had to work at it. She always asked herself if the effort was worth the emotional and mental toll. And in this case, it was. Not just for her unborn child, but for her place in the clan, too.

At least the brief meeting with his sister gave Victoria hope that Jose's family would all accept her eventually.

Maybe.

Jose squeezed her hand in his and said, "It'll be fine, love, you'll see. A dragon-shifter finding his true mate is a huge deal on PineRock, especially since it hasn't been happening as much in the last decade or two."

She glanced at him. "So you mean they'll accept me, even if I am a lowly human?"

He grunted. "You're not lowly."

She'd been half-joking, but his grunt and words made her smile a little. "Thanks. But what I meant was that you didn't exactly seem thrilled when you first entered that ballroom, back in South Lake Tahoe. I had no idea if it was because we were all human or because of the situation."

"Most definitely the situation. I was dragging my feet for the sake of my sister." He brought her hand to his lips and kissed the back of it. "But then I saw you."

There went her belly doing summersaults again.

However, she wanted to know more than just how he felt about one human, so she asked, "Do you interact with many humans, then?"

He shrugged. "My dad and I both work with humans almost every day in the Forest Service. So I've met my fair share. Not all of them are bad."

Realizing how little she knew of her baby daddy, she jumped at the chance to learn more. "What do you do with the Forest Service?"

He shrugged. "Mostly help clear downed or dangerously teetering trees, clean up avalanches or mudslides, and keep an eye out for trespassers or other criminal activity."

"And they trust you and other dragon-shifters to do those things?"

He sighed. "Don't listen to all the rumors, Tori. In most areas, in the US at least, the dragons and humans work together for their community. If nothing else, the economy depends on a good relationship between the two."

Maybe the clan accepting her wouldn't be as insurmountable as she'd first thought. "I had no idea. Dragon-shifters aren't allowed anywhere near Vegas or its suburbs. Something about it scaring away the tourists."

He snorted. "We have the opposite problem here—tourists flock to Tahoe to see us flying in the sky, swimming in the lake, or keep an eye out for a dragon perching on one of the mountaintops. There are even tour groups specifically geared toward dragon sightings."

She blinked. "Really?"

He raised an eyebrow. "Just how much did you research Tahoe and its surroundings before coming here?"

"Er, not much. I mostly was focusing on dragon-shifters in general, not in one particular area. As I mentioned before, I didn't think I'd be picked out of a crowd of two hundred."

He stopped, pulled her close, and kissed her gently.

"You were the only one I wanted in that entire room. Don't forget that."

As she stared into his eyes, her heart rate kicked up. It would be so easy to love such a man.

No. It's too soon. Men tended to flee if a woman mentioned feelings too early, at least in her experience. She needed to take it slow.

He kissed her again before placing a hand at her back and gently pushing her forward to walk again. "Okay, since we're nearly there, it's time for a quiz. Do you remember the names of my immediate family?"

She stood up a little taller. "Gaby, Maria, and Jorge," she stated. "Remembering names and faces is one of my specialties. I'll be fine."

He grinned. "We'll see if that ends up being true. I don't know how much of my family will be here, so there may be a few surprises and a whole lot of new names to learn."

She blinked. "I thought it was just your parents and sister?"

"That's what they told me, but that's unusual for a get-together at their house. Most of my family on Pine-Rock always find a way to drop by. That makes me think some of my aunts, uncles, and cousins will 'accidentally' stop by to meet you."

Victoria groaned dramatically. While her family was small—just her and her parents—she'd had students over the years with large families, ones that would come to a high school play and take up several rows. Maybe Jose's family was like that, which meant the night would take a lot of effort to survive without seeking out some corner to recharge mentally and emotionally. "In that case, I should've taken a longer nap."

He squeezed her waist. "If you get tired, just tell me and I'll get us home ASAP. If you haven't guessed it already, dragon-shifters can be rather overprotective, especially with a mate or a family members' mate. So if any sign of exhaustion shows on your face, the entire Santos family will gather around you, carry you to a bed, and lock the door, standing guard outside until you rest long enough by their standards."

Victoria wasn't entirely sure how to respond to that. Neither of her parents had siblings, just like her.

Even her grandparents had died a number of years ago.

The only other constant person in her life was her best friend, Sasha Wolfe. And since Sasha had three siblings and tons of cousins, her best friend would probably enjoy a large, boisterous family dinner a lot more than Victoria.

However, she was going to give it her best. She may be an introvert unless she was with a very small group of people, but she would try. To try and make a future work with Jose, she'd try. She replied, "I'll make sure to let you know if I need to leave."

As they neared loud music, emanating from one of the older but well-loved houses on the street, she heard

Jose sigh. "There is definitely more than just my parents and Gaby in there."

She looked at the house again, several shadows passing in front of the lit windows covered with curtains.

Her heart sped up, and her palms started to sweat. How could she make a good impression with so many people?

Fight for want you want, Tori.

Doing her best to stand tall, she took a few deep breaths until her heart calmed a little. Drawing on what strength she possessed, she pasted a smile on her face. It was time to pretend she was good with crowds.

JOSE LOVED HIS FAMILY, but right then and there, he wanted to murder a few of them.

Victoria had mentioned to him how she didn't like large groups, and he'd told his parents this.

Apparently they thought the solution was to invite as many family members as possible to prove him and Victoria wrong. It was as if somehow, someway, his family was different from every other group of strangers on the planet.

His inner dragon huffed. *They* are *different, though. They'll try to make her feel welcome.*

Still, that may be too much. Going forward, I need to learn even more about our mate so we can avoid situations like this in the future.

Agreed. His dragon paused a beat before adding, *We could turn back right now, though, if she wants. Let her know that.*

He glanced at Victoria. "We could still leave, and I could tell my parents you're still exhausted from the frenzy."

"No, no, don't do that. I'll be fine for a short while. However, I'll let you know if it becomes too much, and you can sneak me out." She glanced warily at the house. "If that's even possible, given how many people are probably in there, judging by the shadows in the windows."

"Oh, I'll find a way out, love. I promise you that." As he stroked his human's waist, he tried imagining what it was like to be her. Jose, while not the most charming male at first meeting, didn't have a problem with strangers or groups.

Dragon-shifters, in general, had rather nosey and close-knit communities, both out of necessity and tradition. To try and stay away was futile, as almost every teenager learned super quickly.

Victoria glanced back at him with a smile. "I'll just think of it this way—it's more people who can answer my questions about dragon-shifters."

He snorted. "Then go for it. Ask some rather scandalous ones while you're at it. I'd pay to see the reaction of some of my aunts and uncles to anything deemed racy or embarrassing. I don't know, you could ask how instinctual their inner dragons are, especially about sex."

She blushed. "Maybe. Although I have to be careful

about not going too far if I want to make a good impression."

The fact his female wanted to try so hard to win approval made both man and beast stand tall with pride. "They'll love you, just wait and see." They approached the bright yellow house and Jose put a hand on the doorknob. "And here we go."

Opening it, the music grew even louder. It was always a mad scramble for who controlled the playlist for the family get-togethers. The rule was that whoever got their phone connected to the speakers and played music first would have control of it for the entire dinner or gathering.

And judging by the Spanish-language pop music blaring, his cousin Luna had won. Again.

His dragon chuckled. *She does it because it annoys the older ones, but most especially Gaby.*

I know. But it's getting old. I can't remember when someone other than Luna or my sister have won dibs on the playlist.

No sooner had they stepped inside than his mother rushed right up to them, a big smile on her face.

She was only slightly shorter than Jose, which meant she still towered over Victoria. His mother took Victoria's shoulders and then pulled her into a hug. "You must be Tori. My son has told me all about you."

He'd had exactly one fifteen-minute conversation with his mom earlier in the day—dragons didn't call others during a frenzy, so he'd never had the chance before.

But regardless, he'd learned long ago not to waste time correcting his mom on minor things or it could take up an entire evening.

His mother leaned back and studied Victoria. "But he didn't mention how thin you were. Come, I have a table of food for you to choose from. With a little work, we'll get you nice and plump for the baby."

He groaned. "Mom."

His mother raised her brows. "She's human, Jose. That little dragon baby will steal most of her calories if she's not careful. So, yes, she needs to put on some weight."

He glanced at Victoria. At the amusement in her eyes, his irritation eased a fraction. After all, to his mother, cooking was love, and she wanted everyone to have it.

His mate's reaction also meant she didn't offend easily, which should make the night—and blending in with his family—all the easier.

His dragon murmured, *Mom will be good for Tori. They all will.*

Laughter broke out in one of the nearby rooms and his mother looked over her shoulder. "If we don't hurry, my brothers will eat half the table in the next twenty minutes, and the rest will go to my nieces and nephews. And since everyone brought something to dinner, you can have your pick. The more you eat, the more we can learn what you like."

Victoria blinked. "What I like?"

"Of course, Tori. We rotate favorites at our house." His mother frowned. "Even though that can take a while to rotate through, we'll make an exception for you. After all, it's not every day I have a new daughter and a grandchild on the way."

As Victoria stared blankly, no doubt trying to figure out how to handle that statement, Jose stepped in. "Mom, Tori just got here. Let's try to tone down your master life plan until later, okay?"

His mother waved a hand in dismissal. "I don't have a master life plan."

She did—she most certainly did. It involved a dozen grandchildren and her entire extended family moving up from California, Arizona, and Mexico.

With Victoria and his mother's first grandchild being added, his mom would probably find a way to bring the human's family to PineRock, too.

He decided to change the subject so as to not spook his mate. "You could at least introduce yourself to my human before rushing her to the kitchen?"

He silently stared at his mom, telling her not to have Victoria call her mother. Not yet, anyway.

His mom smiled back at his female. "I'm Maria. There, introductions are done. Come, I'll introduce you to my husband, Jorge, after you eat." She leaned closer. "The rest of the family will try to get some words in with you, too, but let me handle them. I'm very good at distracting them when needed."

His mother, the master manipulator.

Too bad it was true, at least when it came to their family

He moved to take Victoria's hand, but his mother came between them. "You've had her all to yourself for weeks. I can have an hour or two."

He was tempted to growl, but Victoria smiled at him. "I'll be okay for a short while. It may be easier to ask those questions you mentioned without you standing at my shoulder."

His mom looked between them. "What questions?"

He ignored her. "Are you sure?"

Victoria nodded. "I'll be fine for a little while."

Jose was torn. A dragon-shifter didn't like to leave their mate's side, especially in the early days after a frenzy. If anything went wrong and she needed a doctor, he wanted to be there to ensure she got the help she needed.

His beast grunted. *But this is our family. They would never hurt her, and we'd trust them with both her life and ours.*

I suppose, he muttered.

He leaned over and kissed Victoria's cheek. "I'll give you fifteen or twenty minutes, then I'm finding you again."

Before his mate could say anything else, his mother guided her away and started chattering.

His sister instantly appeared at his side, almost as if she'd been spying and waiting for him. "It's probably best this way—for Mom to take charge for introductions instead of you doing them."

He glanced at Gaby. "And will you be singing the same tune when you bring your soon-to-be guy around, after your turn with the lottery?"

His sister frowned. "If I'm that lucky."

The lottery contracts were slightly different for the female dragon candidates. They only spent time with the human males for a few days each month—during their most fertile time—and after three months, if there was no conception, the human male never had to see the female dragon-shifter again.

Jose didn't know why the rules were different, nor did he truly understand why his sister had entered in the first place. She'd made it clear for so long that she wasn't ready for children or a mate.

And yet she'd thrown her name into the lottery and nearly begged him to go along with it.

However, weeks of asking hadn't given him answers about her true motives, so he wasn't going to bring it up again. Instead, he lightly bumped his shoulder against her arm. "Well, in honor of my female's first dinner, I think tonight definitely calls for co-opting the music away from Luna, don't you think?"

His sister's eyes lit up with anticipation. "Oh, definitely. Maybe one day Luna will learn to pick something less annoying to play. It wouldn't be so bad, but she picks the same fifteen songs every damn time."

"Then lead the way, little sister. You know how Luna's mind works better than I do, which means you probably know where she keeps her phone."

"I have a few ideas, although she keeps coming up with new ones." Gaby rubbed her hands together in anticipation. "Let's do this."

As he followed his sister to find the secret location of Luna's phone—which controlled the music via a Bluetooth connection to the speakers—his thoughts still went back to Victoria. His mate was being brave, but he hoped it didn't send her into a panic. The Santos extended family was colorful, to say the least.

His dragon huffed. *Have faith in Mom.*

In any other circumstance, he would in a heartbeat. However, his newfound protectiveness was hard to shake off.

Then Gaby picked up her pace and he pushed it aside temporarily. He'd find his mate soon enough. And for the moment, he could work on changing the music to something Victoria could at least understand.

VICTORIA KEPT WAITING for the panic to creep up on her. She'd learned early, at her first kindergarten play in elementary school, that she didn't like being surrounded by strangers. The walls would start to close in on her, it'd get hard to breathe, and she'd eventually freeze up. Time had shown it wasn't merely stage fright, but that it happened anywhere and everywhere.

Only her focus on studying a dragon-shifter up close

for the first time back in the ballroom of that hotel had kept her cool and mostly calm in that crowd.

But as Jose's mother pointed out one relative after another, and most of them waved to her, none of the usual symptoms showed up. Maybe it was because they were dragon-shifters and not humans?

Or, it could just be how most everyone smiled at her and gave some sort of knowing, almost wistful look she couldn't define.

Maria finally pushed her into a large, connected kitchen and dining room. While the actual cooking area wasn't that big, there was a huge table just beyond it, in the dining section. On top of the long, wooden table, card tables were placed along the wall, laden with more food than she'd seen in one place for quite a while.

It was almost like some sort of buffet restaurant.

There was everything from pizza to tamales to plates of fruit, and her stomach rumbled loud enough to be heard above the music.

Maria clicked her tongue. "Let's hurry up and feed you and the baby, Tori. I'll never hear the end of it if the others hear that stomach of yours."

She took a plate, looked at the array of choices, and tried to decide what to eat. After a few seconds, Maria asked, "Don't you like anything here?"

Victoria glanced at Maria. "No, no, that's not it. I just take my time."

She grinned. "Do that here, and you might never eat again."

An older man that looked a lot like Jose, but with threads of silver in his black hair, walked up to Maria and put an arm around her shoulders. A dragon tattoo peeked out from under his short-sleeved shirt. "Some of us have manners, unlike your family, Maria."

Rolling her eyes, she motioned toward the man. "This is my mate and Jose's dad, Jorge."

Jorge nodded at her. "Although my mate isn't completely wrong about if you take too long, you won't get anything. Dragon-shifters tend to eat a lot—you burn a ton of calories when flying—and there never seems to be enough food. Everyone will hold back for now, but as soon as you're not pregnant anymore, then all bets are off."

Both of Jose's parents kept mentioning her pregnancy so casually, despite the fact it hadn't even completely sunk in for her.

For the first time, she wondered if she wasn't already pregnant, would Jose's family have accepted her so readily?

The music suddenly switched to some 90s rock and a woman yelled somewhere, "This is war, Gaby!"

"And the girls are at it again," Jorge muttered. "You think that after they hit twenty, they'd have grown up a little."

That's right—dragon-shifters hit full maturity at twenty. Which, of course, brought up more questions. Needing a distraction from the talk of babies, she blurted, "So if a dragon isn't considered a full adult until twenty, how does that work exactly? Do human laws not cover them off the clan's lands?"

"They do. We have no choice but to follow them, no matter how stupid they are," Jorge bit out.

Maria sighed. "Don't get him started. There isn't much difference at that age, to be honest, when it comes to human and dragon laws. The only main difference is that clans don't allow our matings—the equivalent of marriages—before twenty, just in case a true mate is nearby. Some do mate without finding them, but no one wants to risk the younger ones regretting a rash decision to mate at eighteen or nineteen."

She barely knew Jose's parents, yet she couldn't help but ask, "Do any dragons from PineRock visit the surrounding human cities to look for their mates?"

Jorge shook his head. "Not in recent history, although I suspect Wes wants to change that." Jorge paused as the song turned upbeat, and he smiled. "But this conversation is kind of heavy for a family dinner. Grab some food, Tori, or else my son will start lashing out, wondering why we didn't take care of you."

As she loaded her plate, she warred with that idea. On the one hand, part of her liked the fact Jose wanted to take care of her so badly. On the other, she wondered if it meant she'd never have true freedom again.

Or at least as much freedom as a human mated to a dragon-shifter could have.

"Tori."

Looking up, she met Jose's gaze and everything else

faded away. The warmth and pure joy at seeing him made her heart skip a beat.

As soon as he was at her side and touched her lower back, a sense of peace came over her.

Hm, maybe that's what happened between true mates—everything just came easier.

In the next second, Gaby dashed past, out the back door, and another woman about the same age ran after her. Jose snorted. "Most of my family is behaving. Those two give you a glimpse of what it's like when everyone's not on their best behavior."

She glanced up at Jose. "I look forward to the day when everyone isn't on their best behavior."

Both he and his parents chuckled, but Jose was the one to reply. "You may regret those words one day, love. You just may."

As she leaned against Jose's side and ate a forkful of some kind of rice, she didn't think she would.

Chapter Ten

The next few weeks whirred by in a blur. Victoria spent most of her time in the cabin with Jose or at his parents' house, with a few trips to see the doctor and the head Protector when needed.

Things were too good to be true, and in many ways were like a dream. She had a man curious about her, wanting to learn every little thing, and spoiling her more than she'd ever been in her life. Not to mention she lived with a clan of freaking dragon-shifters. Being able to see a dragon launch into the air at any moment would never get old.

And yet with each day that passed, she waited. Something would have to happen because everything was too damn perfect.

One morning she was getting ready in the bathroom when she heard glass breaking from somewhere inside the cabin. And it sounded more than merely something falling from a shelf—it was as if someone took a sledge-hammer to a window or an entire crate of dishes.

She just caught herself from shrieking and debated what to do. She didn't have her cell phone with her, the tiny window in the bathroom wasn't big enough for her to climb out of, and it wasn't as if she could investigate anything since she wasn't trained in any sort of self-defense or weapons.

Something she was going to work on after today.

So she turned off the shower, dried off and dressed in record time before sitting on the floor with the door locked, and listened closely. However, she didn't hear anything else break or even footsteps walking down the hall.

Still, she didn't want to risk someone lying in wait. Given how much she loved her books, her imagination rattled off one scenario after another, none of them good.

Her best option was to find something to use as a weapon—only as a last resort—and wait for Jose to come home.

With a long-handled wooden bristle brush she used for exfoliation in hand, she waited, sitting on the floor. After a while, her butt started to hurt from the hard tile and her stomach churned, letting her know it was time to eat again.

Even when there could be danger, her little dragon baby wanted food.

At least that was the same, and it helped to keep her

from panicking. If nothing else, no one would hurt her physically until at least the baby was born. That was something she'd learned from her daily lessons—dragon-shifters treasured children.

Yet as the minutes ticked by, she started to reflect on how much she'd left unsaid. If she died today, she would've had a huge regret—not telling Jose how much he'd come to mean to her.

Which meant if she survived the day—she hoped no one would come back—she should find a way to tell him.

Eventually she heard a roar and Jose's voice bellowed through the house. "Tori! Where are you?"

Standing up, it took a second to balance. Ignoring the pins and needles in her feet, she unlocked the door. "Jose?"

He was there within a matter of seconds, holding her slightly back from him by the arms, and checking her out from head to foot. "Are you okay? Are you hurt anywhere?"

Victoria had stayed strong as long as she could, but tears started to trickle down her cheeks. "I-I'm fine, but I heard broken glass. And not like one cup being dropped, but as if an entire crate had fallen."

He pulled her against his chest and gently stroked her back. "I want to calm you down first, love. Then I'll tell you what I saw."

Closing her eyes, she leaned against his chest and breathed in his now familiar scent of pine, dirt, and a musk that was uniquely Jose. "You were clearing trees again today, weren't you?"

"Yes, but that's not important." He kissed the top of her head. "After today, I'm taking more time off."

For a few beats, she allowed the silence, soaking up his strength. Then finally she took a deep breath and lifted her head. "Tell me what happened."

He growled. "Someone broke the front windows. They tossed rocks inside, with notes attached. As well as wrote a message on the front door."

She had a feeling she knew what the message would be, but she forced herself to confirm it. "What did it say?"

"Go home, human. You're not welcome here."

Searching his gaze, she asked, "Is that the true message or a censored one?"

"That's the message, although I'd wager the ones wrapped around the rocks aren't as nice."

She laid her head back against his chest. "I knew everything had gone too smoothly."

"Don't worry, Wes will handle this." He paused and then asked, "I wasn't here to protect you. I'm sorry, love. It won't happen again."

She shook her head. "You can't watch me every second of every day, Jose. Besides, dragon-shifters like strength and fortitude. I'm going to have to learn a way to protect myself and force myself to interact with more than your family, the doctor, Cris, and my tutor."

He growled, "Not until this matter is solved. There's no way in hell I'll let you wander freely, possibly walking right past someone who wanted to harm you."

She met his gaze again, her tears forgotten. "And I'm not stupid, Jose. I stayed in the bathroom, knowing it'd be foolish to come out and try to take care of any sort of intruder on my own. But I need to learn how to defend myself. And before you mention the baby, just know that Dr. Carter says everything is going fine. I won't break from a few basic training exercises, not this early."

"We'll see. Right now, I need to get you to Cris and Wes."

He scooped her up in his arms and she squeaked. "I can walk, Jose. It'll only make me look weaker to be carried by you."

"I won't budge on this, love. And it's not weakness, but a message that if anyone threatens you, then they threaten me and my entire family."

At his flashing pupils, she believed his words were truthful and not merely hyperbole.

Not wanting to poke an already irate dragon, she leaned against her man, soaking up his heat and scent, and tried her best not to gasp at the damage to the front room. The windows were gone and the rocks weren't tiny things, but rather large stones that she probably couldn't even pick up. They'd crushed most of the furniture in the room, and even put a hole in one wall.

And to think, if she'd been in this room, they could've killed her.

So much for dragon-shifters treasuring children. Someone's hatred of her was stronger than protecting her unborn child.

Victoria swallowed and Jose picked his way around the glass and grunted. "So now you understand the danger, right? If they'd killed you..." He trailed off, his eyes flashing even faster, until his gravelly voice continued, "This goes against more than one clan law. And I won't rest until we find out who did it."

ANGER CHURNED INSIDE JOSE, making him want to drop Victoria off with his parents and go find the fuckers who dared to threaten his female.

The second he'd seen the front of the cabin, his heart had stopped beating. It had become crystal clear that Victoria was more than just his true mate or the mother of his child. She was the love of his life, and the thought he would never get to see her smiling face again or to suffer her teasing had created a giant, gaping hole in his heart.

But as he held her close against his chest and kept his eyes and ears out for any more attackers, he knew now wasn't the time to tell his female how he felt. First and foremost, he needed to ensure her safety.

His inner dragon spoke up. *We need to do as she asked and get her trained.*

I know. But if Wes can't let the clan know this is unacceptable and against our laws, then a few self-defense lessons will mean nothing.

Wes will find a way to protect her.

Jose wished he was as confident. Wes had been clan leader for about three years and had yet to face any real trials to his leadership.

Not that Wes was weak or hadn't earned his place. ADDA had difficult trials and interviews to ensure the clan leader would not only be able to keep a group of dragons in check, but also understood the importance of being allied with the American Department of Dragon Affairs.

However, in addition to what had happened today, Jose's sister was right now about to pick out a human male and possibly find another human to stay on Pine-Rock. Wes needed to deal with the discord and violence quickly.

As he walked toward the main security building, Victoria remained silent the entire time and it killed him. She always liked to tease him when alone or ask him questions about his kind.

The silence told him that his brave human was scared. Which made him hold her a little tighter against his body.

Reaching the Protectors' headquarters, he noted the car parked in front of it. *Fuck.* No doubt Ashley Swift was here to check up on Victoria.

He murmured to his mate, "We may have a problem, love. I think Ashley's here."

She looked up at him. "Isn't there a back way into the building? I'm sure Wes can think of a way to delay my meeting with her, even if he has to lie and say I have extreme nausea or something."

"Considering you haven't had any yet, and she knows it, that would only raise red flags. That human is too perceptive."

"We'll think of something."

With a grunt of agreement, Jose went around the back and up the stairs to Cris's private office. He pounded his foot against the door—ignoring Victoria's cries to put her down already—until the head Protector opened the door. She glanced between Jose and Victoria. "What's wrong?"

"Let us in first."

Cris stepped back and let them in before closing and locking the door. Everyone knew her office was sound-proofed and protected from any sort of listening devices or cameras, so Jose said bluntly, "Someone attacked our house and could've killed Tori."

Cris's pupils flashed. "What? Sit down and tell me all the details. Leave nothing out."

Jose eased into one of the two armchairs in front of Cris's desk, keeping Victoria in his lap as he explained the damage and message—he hadn't read the ones on the rocks, wanting to leave the scene as is for the Protectors. When he was finished, Cris cursed and said, "The fact no one reported the incident to me, even with your cabin being in a heavily populated area, worries me more than anything."

He'd thought the same thing, too. "Wes needs to know, and then you need to tell me how you plan to protect my mate."

For all Cris's bravado and borderline arrogance, her gaze turned apologetic toward Victoria. "I'm sorry this happened. I swear I didn't purposely allow someone to possibly kill you."

Victoria nodded. "I know. You've been softening toward me."

Cris rolled her eyes. "Don't push it, human."

When his mate smiled, both man and beast calmed a fraction. If nothing else, she was less afraid and in shock than fifteen minutes ago. "What are you going to do, Cris?" he demanded.

"I'm going to brush aside the dominance in your voice this one time, due to the circumstances. You two are going to stay here and I'll post my second-in-command right outside the door. I know it's hard to wait—especially when your dragon must be demanding heads, Jose—but you need to stay here while Wes and I figure out what to do."

His dragon growled. *Of course I want to catch the bastards, but I won't leave Tori until she's calm again, not to mention safe.*

Agreed. Jose replied to Cris, "We'll stay, but I'll feel better once Dr. Carter checks her over, just to be safe."

Victoria didn't try to deflect, but merely nodded. "I know that'll help calm your dragon, so that's a good idea."

He blinked. His female had been targeted, could've been killed, and here she was, worrying about him and his inner dragon.

He loved her so fucking much it hurt.

And after today, he wasn't going to hide it anymore.

Cris murmured, "I'll leave you two alone for now," and exited the office.

Barely noticing the head Protector's departure, Jose cupped Victoria's cheek and turned her head until her eyes caught his. He murmured, "I know this isn't the time, but I have to tell you, Tori. I love you. The thought of losing you—neither my dragon or I can bear it."

She raised a hand to his jaw, searching his eyes. "I've loved you for a little while now, too, Jose Santos. I just didn't want to scare you off."

He was gentle, but still tightened his grip on her waist with his other hand. "Nothing you could do, short of killing me, will take me from your side."

"Don't even joke about that."

"I'm sorry, love. But it's hard for me to not be out there, seeking retribution, for what was done to you." He leaned his forehead against hers. "Just know that this dragonman isn't going anywhere. You're my female, and I love you with everything I have."

She kissed him. At first, her lips were gentle against

his, but as soon as he could slip his tongue into her mouth, it turned more frenzied. He needed to taste her, feel her, remind both man and beast that his mate was alive and in his arms.

And while kissing her helped soothe his soul a fraction, he wished he could claim her properly, relearning every curve and valley of her beautiful body.

However, vibrations from the door—signaling someone knocking—stopped him from going further. He was about to bark for them to go away, but then remembered they wouldn't be able to hear them.

Victoria murmured, "It's probably for the best. We can celebrate each other later, once we're alone and safe."

He brushed a few strands of hair off her face. "Then I'll just keep telling you how much I love you until then."

Her cheeks flushed. "You say that as if it's some sort of hardship. But it makes my belly flip every time."

He took a quick, rough kiss and said, "I love you, Victoria Lewis."

This time, a chime sounded, a reminder that someone was at the door. She stroked his cheek and then maneuvered off his lap. "That's probably Dr. Carter."

After checking via the peephole and confirming it was, he let the doctor in.

And even though Victoria answered the doctor's questions and did whatever he asked, her gaze kept darting back to Jose. At the love and wanting there, he managed to pace a little less and he could better control the urge to leave the room to find the bastards who'd attacked his home.

It was his job to stay with his mate. He'd trust Wes and Cris to find the culprits.

Chapter Eleven

W es Dalton had always wondered when his first real test as clan leader would come. And of course, when it rained, it fucking poured.

As Cris finished telling him what had happened to Jose and Victoria's cabin and then left him to deal with the ADDA employee, his dragon growled. *We should be going with Cris, not dealing with* her.

The sooner we get her away without raising suspicion, the quicker we can help Cris find the ones who dared risk the wrath of ADDA.

His beast grunted. *Then just tell the human to go away and come back later. Having her around only makes it hard for the pull to fade.*

Ah, yes. The true mate pull. The female didn't know she was his true mate, but he sure as hell did.

Until Victoria had shown up on PineRock, he hadn't seen Ashley Swift in over three years. He'd thought maybe that had been enough time to allow the constant need to kiss her fade. The ability to move on happened with some dragon-shifters, given enough time.

Just not him.

Of course both man and beast still noticed how damn beautiful she was, loving her dark hair and curvy yet tall body. However, her position within ADDA and the law against ADDA employees fucking—let alone mating—dragon-shifters hadn't changed. He couldn't have her, or he'd risk his clan and all the goodwill they'd earned in recent years.

So he'd stayed away. Even his inner dragon had accepted they'd never have her. Or, at least his beast had until the human female had reappeared in their life.

If Ashley kept coming around, Wes wasn't sure what would happen. Inner dragons didn't see the need to hold back as much as the human halves. Constant contact may even put this fairly well-trained dragon to the test.

Pushing thoughts of the female out of his head, he replied to his beast, *The meeting with Ashley will go faster if I put you in a mental prison. That way, your lust won't make it hard to concentrate.*

Fine. But bring me out as soon as she's gone, or next time, I'll fight it.

As much as Wes hated to do it, he constructed a complex prison inside his head and locked his dragon inside.

Maybe now he could solely focus on protecting his clan and not notice the human female.

He pressed a button on his desk, letting his assistant know he was ready for the human. A minute later, Ashley walked into his office at the Protectors' security building.

As her long, dark hair swished behind her as her lush hips swayed, he barely kept his jaw from dropping. Without even trying, she was the sexiest female in the world.

Then her scent bombarded his nose, and he resisted a groan at the clean female scent with only the slightest hint of something flowery.

Even though he wished it wasn't the case, in a room full of people, he'd be able to pick out Ashley in a heartbeat.

The mate he'd never be able to have.

Forget her, he reminded himself.

Somehow he kept his expression free of emotion and stood in greeting. "Since I knew you'd make a fuss if someone else told you my message, I figured I'd just do it myself. You're going to have to come back later, Ms. Swift."

Unfazed as she'd been the first day he'd met her, she raised her brows. "Just because you say something in a dominant tone and treat it as an order doesn't mean I have to follow it, Wes."

Even just hearing his name on her lips made his dragon beat against the mental prison.

Wes needed to get the human away from him, and quickly. He stated, "Victoria isn't feeling well, that's all. She can call you to let you know when she's better."

She studied him a second. "I think you're lying."

How the fuck did she know that? Wes was extremely good at hiding his true thoughts. It was almost a requirement to be clan leader. After all, letting your emotions dance all over your face would only reveal weaknesses to be exploited. "Do you really want to waste time bringing Dr. Carter in to repeat the same information, just because you wanted to display your power over me?"

She crossed her arms over her chest. "I think we should call the doctor. Not because I'm running a power play, but because you're lying, and I want to know why. You may not see Victoria as anything more than a baby machine, but she's my charge and duty. I'm the one tasked with protecting her, and I won't let her down."

Her dedication and loyalty only made him want to rush over to her, pull Ashley against his body, and kiss the living shit out of the human.

She was like his waking dream made real.

No. He wanted to growl in frustration at the impossible, but resisted. He didn't have any other choice. "Look, Ashley, I have something to take care of inside my clan, something that doesn't involve you. If you want to pull your ADDA superiority training out and make this into a contest of wills, I'll win in the end. You know it. So just believe me when I say Victoria is safe"—*for the moment* —"and she'll meet you again in a few days. So leave and go take care of whatever other babysitting duties you have."

She leaned forward, and it took everything he had not to stare at her plumped up breasts.

Fuck, what she did to him. His clan was about to devolve into crisis if he didn't act fast, and here he was, wondering what her naked breasts looked like.

After staring at him a few beats, she uncrossed her arms and sighed. "Fine, I'll go. But have Victoria call me as soon as possible. If I don't hear from her by the end of the day, I'll file a complaint and come back. And next time, I won't leave, either, until I see her." The human turned toward the door but stopped to add, "You're hiding something, Wes. And I'll find out what it is eventually. Remember that."

He was hiding more than one thing, but he remained silent and didn't change his expression.

Ashley finally exited the room, and as soon as the door clicked closed, Wes ran his fingers through his hair and let his dragon out of the cage.

His beast growled. *The more she stands up to us, the more I want her.*

I know, dragon. Me too.

But they could never have her.

After straightening up and taking a few deep breaths, he moved to the monitor at his desk and watched the security feed until Ashley drove out of the tunnel and off PineRock's lands.

The temptation gone, he dashed out of his office, shouting a few things to his assistant, and headed toward Victoria's cabin.

It was time to get the shitstorm under control and put his clan to rights.

Before becoming clan leader, he'd been an investigator of sorts, working with humans to locate missing persons or solve mysteries in the more remote locations that could only really be accessed via helicopter or dragonwing. If he hadn't gone for the clan leadership, he probably would've earned his way into the joint human-dragon police unit for the greater Tahoe area by now, one of only a handful of such cooperations in the entire country.

It may have been a few years since he'd used them, but Wes hoped his skills were still sharp enough. If he didn't solve who had possibly tried to kill the human, and soon, he'd have no choice but to send Victoria to either ADDA or one of the other dragon clans for protection.

And given how happy the female had made Jose, he didn't want to do that. And not just because sending her away could make his dragon go insane, either.

So he picked up his pace and ran, the exercise helping his brain to focus.

After all, the crime was an attack on his leadership, too. And while the humans liked their laws and various warnings via paperwork, dragons needed more. He'd just have to figure out what the hell to do to reach both the human and dragon halves of his clan members.

Chapter Twelve

After Dr. Carter had cleared Victoria's health, three Protector escorts took both her and Jose to his parents' house. No doubt it would've been easier to keep them inside the security building, but there weren't any long-term living quarters inside it. As Victoria and Jose had left, Cris muttered about changing that as soon as she could.

Once they'd finally seen her and Jose inside the Santos's house, the Protectors went to various posts around the perimeter to stand guard.

It seemed Victoria would be stuck inside the house until further notice.

While it was petty to resent it, she'd had so little freedom already. Now she might have even less.

Only Jose maneuvering her to his lap, murmuring how he loved her, kept her from becoming completely worried and a little depressed about their situation. It wasn't every day someone tried to kill you, after all.

Since Jose's parents were both still at work, and Gaby was in South Lake Tahoe getting ready for her own lottery, it was just the two of them.

And for probably the first time in her life, Victoria wished the house was full of people. With a sigh, she said, "I actually miss your family."

She felt his smile against her forehead. "That didn't take long."

"Well, I don't know why, but when I'm around your family, it doesn't feel like a crowd. Maybe because there's always so much chaos, and conversation, and laughter that I don't feel everyone watching me. I still don't know them all yet, at least very well, but no one's said even one harsh word to me. I think that helps, too."

He hugged her tighter against him. "I can invite as many of them over as you like in a little while. However, right now, I just want to hold you and make sure you're okay."

She leaned back to meet his gaze. "That's the thing—just sitting here is making me think of everything that could've happened today, Jose." She turned in his lap to straddle his hips. "What I need is a distraction. Or maybe a mini-celebration of life." She kissed his cheek. "As I sat on that bathroom floor, all I could think about was seeing you and one day, our baby." She kissed his brow. "Remind me of how we're both still alive, and that you're here with me right now."

She placed a gentle kiss on his lips, lingering there, merely reveling in his soft, warm skin.

When Jose finally pulled away, he searched her gaze. "Are you sure, love?"

She raised her brows. "Are you saying you don't need me, too?"

With a growl, he picked her up and carried her to one of the guest bedrooms upstairs. "Don't you ever say that. You're my life, my happiness, my guiding light, Tori. I was trying to be sensitive and understanding, but I think you need a little animalistic dragon-shifter attention. "

At the intensity of his gaze, the heat, the wanting, the desire rushed forth. Her heart rate kicked up. "Yes, I do. I really do."

He sprinted the last few feet to the guest room, shut the door after him and tossed her gently onto the bed. "Tell me you'll stand in front of the clan and officially be my mate under both human and dragon law."

"Yes," she breathed.

He ripped off her top and bra. "Tell me you're mine."

"I'm yours, Jose. Always yours."

Her skirt and panties were next.

Which meant she sat naked on the bed, a sexy as hell dragonman surveying every inch of her body with approval. "Then it's time to pleasure my little mate and show her just how much I need her, want her, can't live without her."

His clothes were gone within seconds. And before she

could do more than blink, he was lying atop her, his hard shaft pressing against her belly as he leaned his head down, his lips nearly touching hers. "I love you, Tori. Always."

Her heart thudded so hard she swore it'd explode. "I love you, too, Jose."

With a growl, he crushed his lips against hers, the kiss no longer gentle but demanding, probing, seeking. It was as if he needed to confirm she was still with him.

And Victoria needed the same.

So she tugged his head even closer, her other hand going to his shoulder and digging in her nails. He growled into her mouth and started to thrust against her, his long, hard cock rubbing deliciously against her throbbing clit.

Her legs fell open even more, and soon she ached to feel him, needing him inside her. She broke the kiss and lifted her hips. "Don't make me wait, Jose."

His pupils flashed quickly, never settling on either round or slitted. She had no idea who was in control, but she didn't care. Victoria loved all of him, inner dragon and all.

He positioned his cock at her entrance, murmured, "Mine," before thrusting deep.

She scratched down his shoulder and moaned, "Oh, yes," before he began to move.

Each thrust of his hips was a claim, a reminder that he was here with her—right here, right now.

His lips never left hers, his tongue nearly as

demanding and aggressive as his cock, plunging, taking, stoking her to a fever pitch.

Then one of his hands found her bundle of nerves and with a few strokes, she crested over the edge, pleasure rushing through her body, making her scream his name into his mouth.

Jose followed, his orgasm sending her even higher, to the delicious point bordering on pleasure and pain. The place only he could send her.

Her mate, her love, the father of her child.

Jose finally collapsed on top of her, at least mostly, being careful not to completely crush her.

She smiled. He'd remembered how she liked feeling his strong, warm body over hers. "I don't think I can ever live without you, dragonman."

He grunted. "Good, because I sure as hell couldn't."

Jose lifted his head, his pupils flashing wildly. She asked, "What does your dragon want?"

"You." He brushed hair from her face. "Can you take him, too?"

"Always."

She'd barely muttered the words before her mate's dragon took over and showed his own brand of love and claiming, making her feel more wanted than she'd ever thought possible.

HOURS LATER, Jose held a sleeping Victoria in his arms,

both man and beast more settled than they'd been earlier.

His inner dragon spoke up. *She's tired because of me. We both know that I wear her out more.*

Why do you say that so smugly? She is carrying our baby, which means you shouldn't try to exhaust her so much.

His dragon huffed. *She's strong, and the doctor said in perfect health. She can handle me. Otherwise, she wouldn't be our mate.*

He watched Victoria's eyes dart behind her eyelids and resisted the urge to trace every curve of her face. *It'll be even better once we make it official in front of the clan.*

What neither of them said was that they could only do it if Wes and Cris found the culprits and settled things down enough for ADDA's approval.

He'd never really thought about how much control ADDA had over their lives before, but he was starting to realize it was far too much.

Maybe that was something Wes could work on, too. The clan leader seemed to have a way with humans that Jose usually didn't, except with his own mate, of course.

Brushing aside the concern and wondering if it were possible for now, he merely watched his female sleep, the sight calming both halves of him.

Jose had no idea how much time passed before his cell phone vibrated in the pocket of his forgotten jeans on the floor. Under normal circumstances, he'd probably ignore it to let his female sleep.

But today wasn't normal, so he slowly slipped out of

bed, fished it out, and noted it was from Wes before answering. "What did you find out?"

Wes didn't bother with any sort of greeting, either. "We found out who did it and have them in custody. Can you and Tori come to the Protectors' main building? I want to talk with you before making my final decision about what to do."

His grip tightened on the phone. "Who is it? Tell me."

"No, because then you'll try to find a way to punish them on your own. And if you succeed, I'd have to issue your punishment, too, and I don't need to lose any more clan members today."

His dragon wanted to roar and say it was their due. However, Jose managed to keep control of their mind and answered, "We'll be there as soon as possible."

Clicking End, he looked over to find Victoria sitting up, awake. "Was that Wes?"

"Yes, and he found out who did it. But don't ask for any more details because he didn't fucking tell me anything."

She stood and went to him. Her hand on his bare chest helped to ease his anger a little. "He's our clan leader, Jose. We need to trust him."

Just her referring to Wes as their leader and not his helped him to rein in his fury. "I know. It's just hard. We may appear civilized, but dragon-shifters are still half animal. The instinct to eradicate threats to our family runs deep." He eyed her torn clothing on the floor. "We need to find you something to wear, though, because Wes wants to meet with us straightaway."

"Your sister is taller and more toned than I am, but maybe she'll have something loose-fitting that'll work."

Jose tugged on his jeans and followed her to Gaby's room. After a few minutes, she found a stretchy dress that fit, as well as some flip-flops that were a little big but good enough, and then they met the Protectors at the front door.

He looked down at his mate. "We'll get there faster if I carry you."

After a beat, she nodded. "Okay, but don't take it as a free pass to do it whenever you feel like it. In the future, ask before you start carrying me around the clan willy-nilly. Otherwise, everyone's going to either think I'm super weak or super manipulative."

He put one hand behind her knees and the other at her back, and lifted. "As soon as people get to know you better, there's no way they'll think those are possible. To be honest, they'll blame it on me being super protective because of your pregnancy."

As he walked, she smiled up at him. "Then maybe I should use that excuse for other things, too."

"Use it for whatever you want, love."

Her brows drew together. "I prefer when you argue a little about it, though. Otherwise, it's no fun."

He snorted. "Sometimes, I don't completely understand you."

She grinned up at him. "That just makes life more interesting."

With the late afternoon sun shining down, high-lighting the reddish streaks in her dark hair, he chuckled. "If I could love you more, I would in this minute."

She leaned against him and laid her head on his chest, saying nothing.

He hated not being able to see her face or read the emotions in her eyes.

But somehow, he knew she needed to hear something. "No matter what happens or what decision Wes makes, I'll find a way for us to stay together, I promise."

"I hope it doesn't come to you needing to think about that." She looked up again. "If we have to leave to stay together, not only will you miss your family, I will, too. Not just for myself, but for our child, too."

He kissed her nose. "Have faith in Wes. He'll make it work."

Thankfully, she nodded and leaned against him again.

Jose only hoped that his words ended up being true. There was a small chance ADDA would take Victoria away until the child was born, give him their son or daughter, and then relocate her to some other part of the US.

And neither man or dragon would accept that fucking option.

Chapter Thirteen

Victoria sat next to Jose at a table in a mostly bare conference room that had light gray walls and no windows. As they waited inside the Protectors' main building for Wes to arrive, she couldn't help but tap her feet.

What was taking so long? It'd been nearly twenty minutes since they'd arrived. And while she was all for wrapping things up and making sure problems were solved, she was anxious to know her future.

The optimist in her said everything would be fine.

And yet, she was learning more and more that dragon-shifters, at least in the US, had to rely a lot on decisions made by the American Department of Dragon Affairs.

The door finally opened, and a frowning Wes entered the room. After one of the Protector guards at the door shut it behind the clan leader, Wes slid into a chair across from them and said without preamble, "Sorry for the wait, but I wanted a confession before meeting with you."

"Did you get it?" Jose asked.

Wes nodded. "The culprits were pretty stupid in the end, and obviously didn't think it through."

Victoria leaned forward. "Please, just tell us who it is and what's going to happen."

Jose wrapped an arm around her shoulder, and she relaxed back into her chair again.

Wes's pupils flashed a few times before he replied, "It was the Randall brothers who did it."

"Who?" she asked, looking between Jose and Wes. There were over a thousand people living inside of Clan PineRock, and she'd barely met any of them.

Wes answered, "The Randall family relocated here a few years ago after a wildfire destroyed their clan in California. They've always kept to themselves, but never caused trouble before."

"But you didn't have a human living here before," she murmured.

"Exactly."

Jose jumped in. "How did you know it was them?"

Wes shrugged. "There were white-blond hairs inside the notes tied to the rocks. Theirs is the only family with hair like that. And while they might've felt tough to threaten a human, they clearly underestimated Cris, the Protectors, and me. They confessed before Cris went to their house and found similar rocks tied with notes, ready for their next attack." Wes's eyes turned dangerous.

"While they haven't admitted it—yet—I think they were hell-bent on continuing until you either left or they killed you."

Victoria resisted swallowing. Wes's tone right then had been that of a guy with which you didn't mess around.

And she sensed he was keeping his anger under control for her.

Never piss off Wes Dalton, she noted.

Jose growled. "What's going to be done to them?"

"As much as I know your inner dragon wants retribution, this is the twenty-first century, which means I have to talk with ADDA." The dread Victoria felt inside her stomach must've also shown on her face because Wes's expression softened, as did his voice. "I'm going to do everything within my power to allow you to stay, if that's what you want, Tori."

Not wanting Jose to speak for her, she nodded and said, "Yes, I do. I know it's going to be hard, and there's still a lot to learn, but as long as you and Cris can keep me safe, I'd like to stay."

Jose tightened his hold on her shoulders a fraction, but she kept her eyes on Wes. If she looked at Jose right now and learned she may have to leave anyway, she'd break down crying.

Wes leaned forward, placing his forearms on the table. "I will do everything to keep you here, Tori. I promise you. But I can't guarantee it."

"I know," she mumbled.

Jose cursed and gently cupped her face to look at him. "We'll find a way to be together, remember?"

Not wanting to argue in front of the clan leader—let alone break down crying—she nodded again.

Wes cleared his throat. "Cris will be by shortly to take official statements. I'll need you to stay here, in case anyone from ADDA needs to talk to you as well." He stood. "I'm going to call them right now and get this whole thing started. The sooner I can get rid of the Randalls by handing them over to ADDA and make an example of them to the clan, the better."

Maybe she should leave her questions for later, but Victoria couldn't bear the not knowing. "What about the rest of the clan? If you fix this, and I'm allowed to stay, what if someone else tries to scare me off?"

Wes's pupils flashed. "We're taking care of that tonight, at a mandatory clan-wide meeting. Cris will give you the details. You both need to attend, but I want to keep you hidden in the back until after I lay down the rules going forward. I don't want to take any chances, especially since no one reported the incident in the first place."

Wes left then, and she let Jose drag her into his lap. As they waited yet again for someone to arrive, Victoria decided she definitely wasn't going to take the future for granted. From tonight, she wanted to get to know as many people from PineRock as possible. Just like humans had misconceptions about dragon-shifters, they probably had them about her kind, too.

And if she wanted the best life possible for her child, she needed to work hard to change things now so that her child wouldn't have to face as many hardships.

JOSE PACED THE SMALL ROOM, the one off to the side of the main stage inside the great hall and wished he could be out there to hear what Wes was saying exactly.

Because whatever it was, it would determine his mate's future and safety.

Victoria grabbed his hand as he walked by, pulling him to a stop. "Wes already worked out some kind of bargain with ADDA for me to stay. Have faith he can do even better with the clan."

"A bargain he won't disclose," he muttered.

His female rolled her eyes. "Don't look a gift horse in the mouth. Or, should I say gift dragon?"

Despite everything going on, his lips twitched. "Who would choose to be a horse over a dragon?"

She leaned against him before looping her hands behind his neck. "I don't know. Horses have it a lot easier. They don't have to worry about people hunting them with pitchforks or swords, let alone crashing into planes if they go too high into the sky. They also get waited on hand and foot."

He grunted. "Exactly. That means they can't take care of themselves."

"But at least I could ride a horse. No one is opening up to my idea about allowing humans to ride dragons."

His dragon snorted. *I'm open to it. After the baby is born.*

Knowing his female would ask, Jose explained, "My dragon says maybe, once the child is born."

"Hm, then I'll remember that. Maybe he and I can come up with some kind of plan when he's in control."

Jose was about to issue a warning to both his dragon and his female when Cris appeared at the doorway. "It's time."

Taking Victoria's hand, he followed Cris out of the room and down a small hallway that lead to the main stage. Cris peeked out a second and then motioned for them to follow.

They exited to a deadly quiet room. All eyes followed both his and Victoria's movements, until Cris had them stop next to Wes, who stood next to a microphone stand.

Cris retreated a few feet, crossed her arms, and Wes finally spoke. "As I mentioned, tonight is a night for celebrations. Everyone here has signed a contract, stating they won't cause harm to any humans that come to our land. As such, you're to witness the first mating ceremony on PineRock between a human and a dragon-shifter in years."

Jose resisted frowning. Wes had them sign a contract? Surely there had to be more to the story, as dragon halves weren't keen on paperwork.

However, as Victoria lightly tugged his hand, he remembered that he was about to mate the female he loved, and she was the only thing that deserved his attention right now.

Wes held up a large wooden box and spoke again. "Inside this are the gifts we give to every newly mated pair, including a set of rings engraved with a unique message written in the old dragon language." He opened the box and held out the rings to Jose. "May your mating be happy, full of laughter, and fruitful."

He took the rings but barely paid them a glance. Jose studied his human, taking in everything about her.

Instead of being afraid or uncertain, despite the fact the crowd inside the great hall had to be one of the biggest she'd faced, she merely smiled at him with love in her eyes.

Needing to make her officially his, he began the ceremony, saying the necessary words. "Victoria Lewis, it's not enough that I love you and want to spend the rest of my life with you. You complete me in a way I never thought possible. When I stood inside that ballroom in South Lake Tahoe, I dreaded trying to pick one female out of the rest. But you stood out immediately, drawing my curiosity and never losing it. You're intelligent, open-minded, kind, and more accepting of my family than I could've ever hoped for." He picked up the small gold band and held it out. "With this ring, I stake my claim, binding us as mates for all time. Do you accept it?"

Without hesitation, she put her finger into the ring and took his hand. "I do."

Releasing his fingers, she picked up the other ring and

cleared her throat. While he could hear her heart pounding, her voice was strong and carried as she said, "I entered the dragon lottery on a whim, merely wanting the chance to learn more about dragon-shifters. I never expected to be selected to participate, let alone have a dragonman pick me out of everyone else. And yet, putting in my application turned out to be the best impulsive decision of my life. You understand me in a way I never thought possible, and I suspect you will continue to surprise me for the rest of my life. And for that, and so much more, I love you, Jose Santos. With this ring, I stake my claim on you. Do you accept?"

He couldn't put the ring on fast enough. "I do."

Wes stepped in, per the custom. "Then, as clan leader, I proclaim you two mates, bound by both human and dragon law, and under PineRock's eternal protection. You may kiss your mate."

Jose pulled Victoria up against his body, loving how she sucked in a breath at the contact, and took her lips with his.

He ignored the cheers and whistles as he licked, explored, and claimed his mate's mouth.

Victoria was his, now and forever.

And once he finally let her up for air, he hugged her even tighter against him and murmured, "I love you, Tori."

She smiled, the sight making him lose his breath. "I love you, too, Jose."

Wes and Cris cleared their throats, breaking the

moment, and Jose growled. "I know, I know, the night's not over yet."

Wes slapped his back and kept his voice low enough that no one else should hear it. "Everyone here is legally bound to accept her, and Protectors are everywhere. I know she doesn't like strangers, but I would highly suggest using tonight to introduce her to as many people as possible, maybe even a few you think she might bond with."

He replied just as quietly, "Still won't tell me your bargain?"

"No. But Tori is safe, and that's all that matters."

His mate leaned forward. "Care to share what all the whisper is about?"

He looked back at his beautiful mate, the curiosity in her brown eyes calming him a fraction. "You remember how I explain the custom, for the newly mated pair to mingle with the rest of the clan, right, and accept their felicitations and/or gifts?"

She sighed. "I do."

He cupped her cheek. "Can you handle it tonight?"

Somewhere in the crowd, his cousin Luna shouted, "Come on, Tori! I want to be the first one to give you a present!"

His mate smiled and murmured to him, "I hope it's not a new playlist."

He chuckled. "Ready to find out?"

She bobbed her head and turned to lean against his

side. "As long as you hold me close, I can handle anything tonight."

He longed to carry his mate out of the room and claim her in their bed.

His dragon snorted. *I'll be the first one, don't worry, so she'll know what a true claiming feels like.*

Not fucking likely, dragon.

Knowing that his dragon would probably fall asleep as soon as he started making the rounds around the room with his female, Jose guided Victoria down the stairs and over to where Luna and the rest of his family stood.

And as he watched his mate smile and laugh with his family, Jose knew he would be the one to claim her, no matter if he had to fight his damn dragon to accomplish it.

Fate had chosen the perfect female for him, and he would never take it for granted. Never.

Epilogue

A *Little Over Eight Months Later*

VICTORIA STARED down at her newborn son and tried her best not to cry. Not because she was sad, but because she was beyond happy.

She'd survived the birth—thanks to shots of dragon-shifter blood—and now had the child that could've been taken away from her if she hadn't fallen in love with Jose and stayed on PineRock.

Jose nuzzled his cheek against hers. "It's okay, love. I'm here, he's here, and soon we'll have more family in the room than you'll know what to do with."

"I-I know." She sniffed. "I'm happy. Truly. It's just the hormones."

He kissed the side of her mouth as he cupped their son's tiny little head, one with more dark hair than she'd thought possible for a newborn. He replied, "I can tell the others to fuck off and give you as much time as you need, Tori."

"No, no, I'll be fine in a moment." She gazed down at the sleeping form of her son. "Let's just give him his name first. As much as I love your family, that's something for only the three of us."

"Agreed." Jose stroked their son's pudgy cheek. "Hello, Liam Alejandro Santos. We've been waiting a long time to meet you."

She leaned against Jose's cheek. "Liam. It's so surreal. After all these months, he's no longer inside me but actually here."

"Given everything that's gone on, I'm just glad things are settled again by the time Liam arrived."

"Me, too."

Between what had happened with Gaby, Wes, and a few others inside the clan—not to mention her own challenges on trying to keep her online teacher gig—the last eight months had been the farthest thing from dull.

But Victoria rather looked forward to things becoming routine. At least, for a short while.

No one knew what the future held, but she wasn't afraid. Regardless of what happened, she would fight for the best future for her son until her dying day.

Liam squirmed a second before falling back asleep.

His actions brought her back to the moment. "You should let the others in, Jose."

"*All* of them?"

She smiled. "Well, maybe not all as that'd be like thirty people. But our parents, your sister, and Sasha, at least."

Sasha Wolfe, her best friend, and one who'd only recently gotten permission to visit.

Never leaving her side, he took out his cell phone. After typing something out, he put it away. "There. If they didn't bring their phones with them, too bad. I'm not leaving your side."

She sighed half-heartedly. The right thing would be to send him out to get their family and friends, but Victoria didn't want Jose to leave her and Liam just yet.

So for the next minute or so, she stared at her son and tried to memorize the moment so she'd remember it always.

Then the parents and best friend entered, and she did her best to smile.

As she watched her son being passed from one person to the next, Jose hovering to ensure they held him correctly, she smiled for real. She had the love of her life, a new child, and the support of everyone who mattered to her.

All that was left was to fight for the best future for her clan and her family. And that fight would be easy as long as she had Jose by her side.

Thank you for reading! I hope you loved Jose and Tori. The next story in the Tahoe Dragon Mates series will be *The Dragon's Need* (about Jose's sister Gaby), which releases March 26, 2020. (And don't worry, Wes and Ashley's story is the third book in the series!) Gaby wants something other than an overprotective dragon-shifter, and enters herself into the Tahoe dragon lottery to take her chances with a human. Once she picks a male, the only question is whether her dragon will scare him off or not…

Preorder THE DRAGON'S NEED now on Amazon US and see what happens on March 26, 2020! (Not in the USA? Amazon UK / Amazon AU / Amazon CA / Amazon DE)

Want a longer dragon-shifter story set in England? Then try the first book in my Stonefire Dragons series, *Sacrificed to the Dragon*. Melanie offers herself to a dragon clan in order to save her brother's life. However, her assigned dragonman is broody and hates humans…

Order SACRIFICED TO THE DRAGON now on Amazon US! (Not in the USA? Amazon UK / Amazon AU / Amazon CA / Amazon DE)

I appreciate your help in spreading the word, such as by

telling a friend about this book. Reviews also help readers find books! Please leave a review on your favorite book site. You can also sign-up to my newsletter for information, releases, and more.

Turn the page for a little more information on both *The Dragon's Need* and *Sacrificed to the Dragon*...

The Dragon's Need

TAHOE DRAGON MATES #2

Tired of overprotective dragon-shifters, Gabriela Santos decides she wants to lose her virginity to a human male via the Tahoe area dragon lottery. After years of trying, she's finally selected as one of the participants. Of the hundreds of humans who want to be with her, it's the male staring at the ceiling who catches her eye. And after a bit of honesty and insight into why he's there, she picks him. However, soon one kiss changes her future forever.

Only to try and forget his cheating ex-wife does Ryan Ford agree to enter the dragon lottery. He has no expectations of the dragonwoman walking the aisles to pick him. However, when his mind wanders and he becomes lost in thought, the dragon lady calls him out on it. Her straightforward manner and wit is refreshing. Add in the instant spark between them, and Ryan agrees to sleep with her to try to give her a baby. But then one kiss brings out her inner dragon, and Ryan quickly learns that he's her true mate and has to accept a frenzy or try running away.

As the pair come to terms with their fate, they soon start falling for one another. But when someone targets Ryan, will he survive and find a way for them to be together? Or will he have to leave both Gabriela and his unborn child to stay alive?

NOTE: This is a quick, steamy standalone story about fated mates and sexy dragon-shifters near Lake Tahoe in the USA. You don't have to read all my other dragon books to enjoy this one!

Preorder THE DRAGON'S NEED now on Amazon US and see what happens on March 26, 2020. (Not in the USA? Find it on Amazon UK / Amazon AU / Amazon CA / Amazon DE)

Sacrificed to the Dragon

STONEFIRE DRAGONS #1

In exchange for a vial of dragon's blood to save her brother's life, Melanie Hall offers herself up as a sacrifice to one of the British dragon-shifter clans. Being a sacrifice means signing a contract to live with the dragon-shifters for six months to try to conceive a child. Her assigned dragonman, however, is anything but easy. He's tall, broody, and alpha to the core. There's only one problem—he hates humans.

Due to human dragon hunters killing his mother, Tristan MacLeod despises humans. Unfortunately, his clan is in desperate need of offspring to repopulate their numbers and it's his turn to service a human female. Despite his plans to sleep with her and walk away, his inner dragon has other ideas. The curvy human female tempts his inner beast like no other.

Order **SACRIFICED THE DRAGON** now on Amazon US and see what happens! (Not in the USA? Find it on Amazon UK / Amazon AU / Amazon CA / Amazon DE)

Author's Note

I hope you enjoyed Tori and Jose's story! This series represents two firsts for me—my first dedicated paranormal novella series and the first adult dragon story that I've designed the cover for by myself. I suppose there's another first, too, in that it's my first set of dragon-shifter stories set in the USA. (If you haven't read them, my other dragon stories are all set in the UK and Ireland.) The idea for the Tahoe series actually came to me while I was "hiking" around Lake Tahoe on my treadmill. The scenery reminded me of the only time I had the privilege to visit Tahoe, about twenty years ago, and how beautiful it was. I could easily see dragons swooping over the lake, or diving in for a swim. The idea for Tori and Jose's story came soon after, and I wrote *The Dragon's Choice* in less than three weeks. (Which, for me, is super fast.) The novella format is fun in that everything goes at a much faster pace. It's also great when you want something that you can read in a day or maybe two. I hope my readers enjoy this format as much as I did writing it.

For the time being, I have a total of three books planned for the Tahoe Dragon Mates series. However, if enough readers are interested and sales are strong, it's possible I could extend it a few more since there are plenty of clans and characters to play with. So if you like this series then make sure to spread the word and/or leave a review!

And now I have some people to thank for getting this out into the world:

- To Becky Johnson and her team at Hot Tree Editing. They always find a way to squeeze me in on short notice, not to mention catch the tiniest inconsistencies.
- To all my beta readers—Sabrina D., Donna H., Sandy H., and Iliana G., you do an amazing job at finding those lingering typos and minor inconsistencies.

And as always, a huge thank you to you, the reader, for either enjoying my dragons for the first time, or for following me from my longer books to this series. Writing is the best job in the world and it's your support that makes it so I can keep doing it.

Until next time, happy reading!

PS—To keep up-to-date with new releases and other goodies, please join my newsletter here.

Also by Jessie Donovan

Asylums for Magical Threats

Blaze of Secrets (AMT #1)

Frozen Desires (AMT #2)

Shadow of Temptation (AMT #3)

Flare of Promise (AMT #4)

Cascade Shifters

Convincing the Cougar (CS #0.5)

Reclaiming the Wolf (CS #1)

Cougar's First Christmas (CS #2)

Resisting the Cougar (CS #3)

Kelderan Runic Warriors

The Conquest (KRW #1)

The Barren (KRW #2)

The Heir (KRW #3)

The Forbidden (KRW #4)

The Hidden (KRW #5)

The Survivor / Kajala Mayven (KRW #6 / 2020)

Lochguard Highland Dragons

The Dragon's Dilemma (LHD #1)

The Dragon Guardian (LHD #2)

The Dragon's Heart (LHD #3)

The Dragon Warrior (LHD #4)

The Dragon Family (LHD #5)

The Dragon's Discovery (LHD #6)

The Dragon's Pursuit (LHD #7)

The Dragon Collective / Cat & Lachlan (LHD #8 / TBD)

Love in Scotland

Crazy Scottish Love (LiS #1)

Chaotic Scottish Wedding (LiS #2)

Stonefire Dragons

Sacrificed to the Dragon (SD #1)

Seducing the Dragon (SD #2)

Revealing the Dragons (SD #3)

Healed by the Dragon (SD #4)

Reawakening the Dragon (SD #5)

Loved by the Dragon (SD #6)

Surrendering to the Dragon (SD #7)

Cured by the Dragon (SD #8)

Aiding the Dragon (SD #9)

Finding the Dragon (SD #10)

Craved by the Dragon (SD #11)

Persuading the Dragon / Zain and Ivy (SD #12 / May 14, 2020)

Stonefire Dragons Shorts

Meeting the Humans (SDS #1)

The Dragon Camp (SDS #2)

The Dragon Play (SDS #3)

Stonefire Dragons Universe

Winning Skyhunter (SDU #1)

Transforming Snowridge (SDU #2)

Tahoe Dragon Mates

The Dragon's Choice (TDM #1)

The Dragon's Need (TDM #2 / March 26, 2020)

The Dragon's Bidder (TDM #3 / Summer 2020)

About the Author

Jessie Donovan has sold over half a million books, has given away hundreds of thousands more to readers for free, and has even hit the *NY Times* and *USA Today* bestseller lists. She is best known for her dragon-shifter series, but also writes about magic users, aliens, and even has a crazy romantic comedy series set in Scotland. When not reading a book, attempting to tame her yard, or traipsing around some foreign country on a shoestring, she can often be found interacting with her readers on Facebook. She lives near Seattle, where, yes, it rains a lot but it also makes everything green.

Visit her website at: www.JessieDonovan.com

Made in the USA
Middletown, DE
18 December 2021

56442138R00106